Cream Caramel and Murder

Holly Holmes Cozy Culinary Mystery – book 1

K.E. O'Connor

K.E. O'Connor Books

CREAM CARAMEL AND MURDER

First edition. March 1, 2021.

Copyright © 2021 K.E. O'Connor.

ISBN: 978-1916357303

Written by K.E. O'Connor

Edited by Amy Hart

Cover design by Stunning Book Covers

Beta read by my wonderful early review team. You're all amazing.

Chapter 1

The chain on the old-fashioned bicycle I rode rattled as I pushed harder. My heart felt like it might burst out of my chest as I leaned over the handlebars. I dug in and eyed the crest of the hill like it was the top prize in a 'win a giant cake' competition.

"Come on, Holly. One small hill won't beat you," I muttered under my breath.

"Woof woof." Meatball turned his head and looked at me from the safety of his basket on the front of the bike.

"That's right. We've done this journey plenty of times. The fact we're pulling what feels like several tons of cake won't defeat us." Cakes I'd lovingly made this morning in the kitchen of Audley Castle.

I puffed out a breath and blew it upward to try to unstick the sweaty dark hair from my forehead.

I wouldn't slow down or take a break. Mayor Baxter needed his cakes for his afternoon tea party, and I wouldn't let him down.

I lifted a hand and waved as I passed Miss Emily Spixworth's cottage, the door framed by a cascade of beautiful flowering giant pink roses. She stood by the front door, wearing a wide-brimmed hat and gardening gloves, admiring her flowers.

She smiled at me. "Good afternoon, Holly. You've got a load there."

"For the Mayor's party," I said. "I can't stop."

She waved me on. "Have fun."

Fun! Well, I suppose this was a free form of exercise, and using the bike meant I'd never need to join a gym in order to stay fit.

It was one of those ridiculously cute, old-style bikes, with no gears and a wicker basket on the front.

The basket was perfect for Meatball, my beloved dog. As a small corgi cross, he fit perfectly inside. He wore a harness and leash attached to the basket, and a specially designed doggie cycling helmet in a fetching blue, just like mine. Safety first when it came to my favorite little guy.

Meatball loved to go on bike rides with me and was always happy to take in the beautiful sights of Audley St. Mary, where we'd lived for just over a year. He often hung his stubby front paws over the basket and let his ears blow back in the breeze, joy on his furry face as we zoomed about the village.

I made it to the top of the hill and smiled. It was plain sailing all the way down.

We passed a small woodland and flew over the bridge across the river. I still pinched myself most days that I lived in this idyllic, pretty piece of heaven. Not only that, I got to live in Audley Castle. How's that for a dream residence?

I slowed the bike as we reached the small parade of shops in the center of Audley St. Mary. I rested my foot on the ground and sighed as I looked at the empty store.

It had once been mine. My own little café. And I'd done well for nine months, tempting people in with my delicious home-made cakes and frothy coffee. It had been a real community hub.

That was until a chain café, which shall not be named and never entered, had opened at the other end of the street.

I'd tried so hard to keep my business going, but I couldn't compete with their special offers and membership discounts. The tourists who frequented the village always went there. It was cheaper, and they recognized the name. They must have been happy to drink weak coffee and eat the stale cakes on offer.

I shook my head. There was no need to be bitter. I'd done my best. The cakes they sold were probably adequate.

"Look, Meatball! It's been sold." I slid off my bike and peered through the soaped over window of the empty store.

"Woof woof." Meatball tilted his tan head from side to side, his ears pricked.

"Yes, it is sad." I patted the window frame like it was my favorite old dog. "Still, we gave it our best shot. And if I still had this café, I wouldn't have taken the job at Audley Castle."

I'd only been working in the kitchens in the castle for three months and was still learning the ropes. The surroundings were beautiful, and most of the staff were amazing, but I'd yet to crack the cool veneer of the strict and imposing Chef Heston. He delighted in yelling at everybody. It was his default setting. The louder he yelled, the harder people worked. That was his theory, anyway.

Although the hours were long, and the pay wasn't amazing, the fact I got to bake every single day more than made up for it. Plus, I got to live in a castle. Well, almost.

Audley Castle was a stunning early seventeenth-century building, designed in a Jacobean style with striking stone cladding. The gardens had been designed by no less than Capability Brown, and there were over a hundred rooms inside and antique furnishings everywhere. It was a beautiful home.

Don't get me wrong, I didn't actually have a room in the castle, but my job came with accommodation set in the beautiful grounds, in a tastefully converted cow shed. It was basic, but it suited Meatball and me just fine.

He whined and leaped up in the basket, resting his paws on the edge. It was a sign he wanted to get out and explore.

"Oh, no. No walk just yet. We've still got these cakes to deliver before we get to have fun." After a final look at my old café, I hopped back on the bike and cycled the last half a mile to Mayor Baxter's elaborate detached house with its thatched roof and wild flower garden.

Climbing off the bike, I hurried along the path to the front door. I knocked, before returning and beginning to unload the cakes from the trolley attached to the back of the bike.

Normally I'd have used the delivery van for such a large amount of cake, but we only had one at the castle at the moment, and Chef had insisted I use the bicycle.

I got the impression that he made me use the bike for his own amusement. He told me that people liked to have their cakes delivered the old-fashioned way. Apparently, seeing me arrive on a bike reminded them of the old days, when people had time to stop and chat and not race back to their van and hide behind the wheel.

They might, but I had to be extra careful not to bash the cakes around on the journey. And when using the bike, I'd often end up a hot sweaty mess in front of some esteemed members of the local community. That was never a look to aspire to.

Audley St. Mary was a stunning place, and that meant houses came with a hefty price tag and attracted a certain class of people.

"Holly Holmes!" Mayor Baxter stood at the front door as I turned back to the house. "I'm delighted you could bring the cakes."

I hurried back with four carefully balanced boxes of cake in my arms. "Of course. We're always happy to help. Where would you like these?"

"Straight through to the kitchen, same as always." He wore his red mayoral ceremonial robes and his official chains of office around his neck. That meant an important guest was arriving.

I'd been to his house several times to make deliveries and had even convinced him to open my café with a ribbon cutting ceremony. Mayor Baxter was a kind man, a little out of touch at times, but his heart was in the right place.

"How are the Duke and Duchess?" He followed me into the expansive marble and granite kitchen that filled a large extension on the back of the house.

"Both well," I said. The Duke and Duchess of Audley had lived in the castle for decades. It had been their ancestral home for over two-hundred years. They were generous benefactors to the village, ensuring the area flourished under their careful gaze.

"I keep meaning to drop by and take the Duke up on his offer of some trout fishing. The trouble is, I'm so busy entertaining." He patted his round stomach. "Not that I'm complaining. Although I do wish you'd make your cakes a little less delicious. I can never resist a second or even a third helping."

I chuckled as I placed the boxes down. "I'm glad to hear it. I've put some of your favorite caramel cream topped cupcakes in today. Who are you entertaining this afternoon?"

"Three mayors from different counties, their wives, and their assistants. We're talking about setting up a charitable foundation. The trouble is, one of them wants to support farmers, another wants to support wildlife, and I want to help prisoners. I thought, given the work already happening at Audley Castle with your excellent rehabilitation program, it would be a perfect fit. I suspect we'll go around in circles for several meetings before abandoning the project because we can't come to an agreement."

"They all sound like worthy causes," I said. "I'll go grab the last few boxes of cake."

"Right you are." He was already sneaking open one of the boxes and peering inside.

I was mostly self-taught when it came to baking. Although I'd completed two years part-time at a catering college, so I knew how to whip up a good cake.

I also had a love for exploring old recipes and was experimenting with a Roman honey bread that was testing my skills. My last three efforts had been too hard to eat. I was missing a vital ingredient, but I had yet to discover what it was.

I returned with the rest of the cakes to find Mayor Baxter licking his fingers. He grinned when he saw me. "You see, I can never resist your cakes."

"We're always happy to provide cakes for you, Mayor," I said as I set the boxes down.

"Are you busy at the castle today?"

"Always. We've got several coachloads of tourists turning up this afternoon. In fact, I need to get back. There's more baking to do before the end of the day."

"Absolutely! Don't let me keep you." He grabbed a cake out of the box and handed it to me, along with a twenty pound note. "That's for you. For all your hard work."

"Thanks! You don't have to do that." It wasn't uncommon to get tips when I made a delivery, but few were as generous as the mayor. The tips went into my recipe savings pot so I could buy more cook books and maybe take a few courses when I had the time.

"Of course I do. Only the best for the most amazing baker in Audley St. Mary."

I nodded my appreciation as I tucked the tip into my pocket. Some people said Mayor Baxter was on the stuffy side, but he was a nice old guy. He didn't let his position as mayor go to his head and was always happy to chat.

"Thanks again. I'd better get going. Enjoy your tea party."

"No doubt we will." He said goodbye as I headed out the front door and back to the bike where Meatball sat waiting patiently in the wicker basket.

I pushed the bike a short way along the lane and stopped by a bench. I unclipped both our helmets and scooped Meatball out, getting a lick on the cheek as a thank you.

I set him on the ground. "Let's have a ten-minute break before we get back to work."

The journey to Audley Castle would be easy now I wasn't towing the cakes and worrying about hitting a pot hole and sending them flying.

Secretly, I enjoyed the bike rides. It was such a pretty village, and the people were so friendly. I was glad this was my home. Even though my business hadn't worked out the way I'd hoped, I'd landed on my feet by getting the job at Audley Castle.

I bit into the delicious cream caramel frosted cupcake Mayor Baxter had given me and sank back against the seat.

Meatball snuffled around my feet, and I extended his leash so he could wander about and have a good sniff.

I'd gotten Meatball from a rescue center when he was a scraggly sad-eyed puppy. It had been just me and him for a long time. We'd even developed our own language. Well, I say language. I was certain that when he barked once, it meant no, when he barked twice, it meant yes, and when he barked all the time, it meant trouble was coming, or to look out because something was happening that he was uncertain about.

Some people thought I was crazy for believing I could talk to my dog, but there was something in it, and it worked for us.

I ate my last piece of cake and licked frosting off my fingers before standing. "Time to get back home." I scooped Meatball into my arms and gave him a quick cuddle before settling him back in the basket and attaching our helmets.

I smiled as I turned the bike around. Life was good. Work kept me busy, I was happy with Meatball by my side, and I was making new friends at the castle, including Princess Alice.

Who'd have thought my new best friend would be a princess? She was something like thirty-fifth in line for the throne, so I really was hanging out with royalty.

I sang as I pedaled back toward the castle. Could I sing well? No! But I enjoyed doing it and had no plans to stop if I was in the mood.

Meatball turned, and his eyes narrowed before he started to howl.

I could never be certain if he was happy howling or unhappy howling thanks to my off-key singing.

I laughed as we reached the top of the hill and let my feet slide off the pedals as we freewheeled down, the wind catching my hair and making it fly out behind me.

We shot around a bend, the small woodland on my left a blur of brilliant green. We'd be back at the castle in less than twenty minutes at this rate.

My eyes widened, and I slammed on the brakes as someone stepped out in front of me. The bike skidded, and my breath caught in my throat as I saw who I was about to hit.

"Lord Rupert! Get out the way!" The back wheel lifted off the ground as I was flipped over the handlebars. I flew through the air and landed on top of him.

The bike clattered behind me, and my heart raced as my brain caught up with what had just happened.

I lifted myself off of Lord Rupert, who'd helpfully cushioned my fall. I looked down at his face, and my heart skipped a beat. His eyes were closed.

I'd knocked him out! Or maybe worse.

"Oh my goodness! I'm so sorry." I patted his cheek. "Lord Rupert, are you okay?"

That was a ridiculous question. Lord Rupert Audley, thirty-fourth in line to the throne, had just been jumped on by a ten stone (and a few generous pounds) woman who couldn't control her bike properly.

"Holly! What have you done?" Jenny Delaney rushed out of her cottage opposite the woods, a dish cloth in her hand.

I pushed myself up, my stomach churning as Rupert remained unresponsive. Just how hard had he hit the ground?

"My word!" Jenny peered with wide eyes at the scene. "That's Lord Rupert."

"Um, yes. He just stepped out. I couldn't stop in time." I leaned over him, willing him to be okay.

He didn't stir.

"I'd better call for an ambulance. And the police," Jenny said as she turned back to her cottage. "I think you've killed him!"

Chapter 2

I scrambled to my feet, staring in horror at the unconscious Lord Rupert. My hand reached for his wrist. I couldn't have killed him.

My breath whooshed out. His pulse was strong, if a little fast.

"He's not dead," I said as Jenny returned from her cottage.

"Are you certain about that?" She stared at Lord Rupert. "Is he even breathing?"

"Yes! I'm sure he is."

Her head shifted, and she frowned. "Your bike is ruined."

"Meatball!" I turned and raced back to the bike. It lay on its side. Meatball was still attached to the wicker basket which had come loose from its fitting.

I grabbed him and unclipped his leash, so grateful I'd invested in his doggy helmet and trained him to wear it. "Are you okay?"

"Don't mind the dog! What about Lord Rupert?" Jenny yelled.

Meatball shook out his fur and blinked at me several times. "Woof woof."

I ran my hands over him to check for any injuries. He was fine, just a bit dusty and shaken up.

Jenny continued to flap around Lord Rupert. "I'm not sure he is breathing, you know."

I hurried back to Lord Rupert's side with Meatball tucked under one arm. I knelt beside him and checked the pulse in his neck this time. I let out a sigh. He was still very much alive, but must have taken a whack to the head when he went down.

I tapped his cheek again. "Lord Rupert. It's Holly Holmes. Can you hear me?"

He still didn't respond. There was an open book of poetry laying by his side.

I sighed and shook my head. He always had his nose in a book and was well known for walking around the village reading. No wonder he didn't see me.

There had been no way I could have avoided him, but I did feel a little guilty. I had been going fast around the bend and wasn't completely in control of the bicycle.

An SUV raced around the corner and stopped beside us. It was a huge, sleek black vehicle with tinted windows so you couldn't see who was driving.

Still, I recognized the vehicle, and my stomach tightened. It was driven by the castle's private security team.

Of course, I should have expected them to be nearby. Whenever any member of the household left the castle, they were accompanied by a discreet security presence to ensure their safety. It was a shame they hadn't been close enough to stop this unfortunate accident.

The driver's door opened. Campbell Milligan slid out of his seat. He was usually assigned to protect Princess Alice, but it looked like he was also covering Lord Rupert's back today.

Campbell was forty-five, clean shaven with dark hair, and had an air about him that reminded me of James Bond. He was tall, broad, and very terrifying.

He strode over, his eyes hidden behind wraparound black sunglasses. "What happened?"

I stood back, clutching Meatball. "Lord Rupert got in the way of my bike."

He knelt over him and checked his pulse. "You hit him?"

"We sort of hit each other." I gestured to my abandoned bicycle. "I came around the corner and he appeared from out of the trees. He was right in front of me."

"Saracen, call for an ambulance," Campbell said to a member of his team who had stepped out of the vehicle.

"There's no need," I said.

"There's every need," Campbell said.

"No, I mean, Jenny's already called for an ambulance."

Campbell glanced at Jenny before running his hands over Rupert's arms and legs. "Nothing's broken."

"I … erm, I did land on him rather hard," I said.

His eyebrows rose over the top of his sunglasses. "This just gets better."

I bristled at his tone. "I didn't do it deliberately. Lord Rupert was reading that book when he stepped out from the trees. I couldn't stop in time, and he didn't even see me. Before I knew it, I was pitching over the handles of the bike and slammed into him. He must have hit his head when he fell."

"He wouldn't have hit his head at all if you'd been in proper control of your bike."

I scowled at Campbell. "You know what Rupert's like."

"That's Lord Rupert to you."

I gritted my teeth and tried to keep my cool. There were dungeons in the castle. I wouldn't put it past Campbell to shove me down there for doing this. "All I'm saying is that it was an accident."

"So you claim." He stood. "I'll have to run a more thorough background check on you if you're going to start assaulting members of the household."

I jammed a hand on one hip. "There's nothing dodgy about me." I'd had a security check before joining the royal household, yet Campbell was looking at me as if I'd just announced I'd planned to blow up the castle.

Jenny inched closer. "How is he?"

"Alive," Campbell said.

"I was in my kitchen, looking out the window. I saw you smash into him," Jenny said.

"By mistake! I hit Lord Rupert by mistake. Better that I land on him than the bike." I felt like I was being ganged up on.

"Didn't you have your feet off the pedals?" Jenny asked. "You didn't look in control of the bike."

I deliberately didn't meet Campbell's gaze. "I don't remember."

"Not only have you injured a member of the household, you also damaged their property by your reckless behavior," Campbell said.

I sighed and pressed my lips together. There was no use trying to reason with Campbell. It was like talking to a brick wall when he was in official security mode. Even when he wasn't, he barely spoke to me. The man was an island. A big, scary, dangerous island I tried to avoid.

Lord Rupert groaned and his blue eyes flickered open. "Oh dear! I appear to be on the ground."

"Stay where you are, sir," Campbell said. "You may have hit your head."

Rupert completely ignored him and tried to sit up. "Holly! That was you! I only saw you at the very last second."

Ignoring the death stare Campbell sent me, I knelt next to Rupert. "I'm so sorry for hitting you."

"That was entirely my fault." Rupert brushed down his dusty dark pants. "I was immersed in the wonders of Wordsworth. Have I ever read you one of his poems?"

I suppressed a smile. "Once or twice."

He ran a hand through his messy blond hair. "Of course. You're always kind enough to spare me a few moments to listen."

I'd met Rupert on my first day at Audley Castle. I'd noticed a tall, blond-haired man wandering around the gardens waving his arms in the air. My curiosity had gotten the better of me and I'd gone to investigate. I'd discovered him reciting poetry to himself.

Rupert had the most wonderful, deep voice, and his pronunciation of every word was perfect. I could listen to that voice for hours; it was mesmerizing, as were his bright blue eyes.

He'd caught me listening and introduced himself. Since then, whenever we bumped into each other and he was reading poetry, he'd often read me a few lines.

"Let me help you up." I extended a hand.

"I'll do that," Campbell said. "And you shouldn't move, sir. You could have a head injury."

Rupert waved a hand at Campbell. "Nonsense. I feel fine." He touched the back of his head and winced. "I've received bigger bumps playing rugby with my friends. This is nothing."

Reluctantly, Campbell helped him to his feet. "Do you feel dizzy or sick?"

"I'm perfectly well. There's no need to worry." Rupert looked at me. "And once again, this is all my fault. You weren't hurt, were you? You landed quite heavily on me."

My cheeks grew warm. "No! You were the perfect cushion to land on."

Campbell snorted and looked away.

"I'm happy to be of service." Rupert rubbed the back of his neck and grinned. "You have permission to land on me any time you like."

I bit my bottom lip and looked away. Rupert wasn't a natural flirt, but I sometimes wondered if he attempted it on me.

"Sir, we need to get you medical attention," Campbell said. "The ambulance is taking too long. I will take you to the family doctor."

"There's no need," he said. "I feel fine. I'm glad I literally bumped into you, Holly."

"You are?" I asked.

"I've got a small private party joining me tonight for a long weekend. Some of the Eton boys are getting together to reminisce about the good old school days. I know it's horribly short notice, but would you be able to cater for us?"

I sucked in a breath. We had a full schedule of work booked in the kitchen already, but I didn't like to refuse him. "Perhaps you should speak to Chef Heston. I'm sure he can provide everything you need."

"I've no doubt he'll come up trumps when it comes to the savories, but you always do something magical with your desserts. I insist you cater the sweet treats. Of course, only if you have time. I've been meaning to speak to you for days, but I've been distracted."

No doubt by the recent delivery of a large crate of new poetry books that had arrived at the castle just a week ago. "Of course, I'm sure we can work something out."

"That would be excellent," he said. "I've told my friends how incredible your baking is. It's only fair they try it for themselves. It's a small party. There will be me, Anthony, Simon, Christian, and Kendal. Five in total, and they love a good spread. I know they'll enjoy your desserts."

"I'm happy to help," I said.

Campbell cleared his throat. "Sir, we really do need to get you to the doctor."

Rupert sighed. "Is that really necessary?"

"It is, sir."

Rupert shrugged at me. "Very well. We should take Holly too. She didn't half fly off her bike."

I shook my head. "There's no need. Other than a scraped knee, I got off lightly."

"Oh! Well, if you're sure. Promise me you weren't injured."

"I promise."

Rupert looked me over before nodding and being led to the back of the black SUV.

"I'll see you later with the food," I said.

Rupert raised a hand before he slid into the vehicle. The door was shut behind him by Saracen.

I placed Meatball on the ground and lifted the bike. "I don't suppose there's a chance of a ride back?" I asked Campbell.

He glanced at the twisted bike wheel and a smirk slid across his face. "You can't ride with a member of the family. You'll have to make your own way back to the castle." He climbed in the SUV with Saracen, spun the vehicle around, and drove off.

"Thanks so much for your help!" I scowled at the retreating vehicle.

Jenny, who'd been standing to one side watching the show, raised a hand. "I'm glad no one was killed. Maybe you should slow down, though."

I sighed. I had no doubt this little drama would be all over Audley St. Mary by the end of the day. Small places like this had wickedly good gossip grapevines. "Thanks for the advice. Come on, Meatball. We need to get back to work. We've got baking to do."

Chapter 3

"Are you certain Lord Rupert said he wanted you to make all the desserts?" Chef Heston fluttered around me, peering down his long nose and pressing his lips together as he stared into my mixing bowl.

"He did." I mixed up the chocolate sponge cake batter and poured it into individual paper cases.

"Why you?" He looked almost green with envy, his chin jutting out and his dark eyes narrowed.

I hurried to the oven and slid the cakes in before shutting the door and setting the timer. "Lord Rupert likes my desserts. But you're in charge of everything else. That's most of the meal we'll serve tonight. I'm only doing the pudding."

His top lip curled. "You seem to forget yourself. I'm in charge of this whole kitchen, including the hiring and firing of staff who don't toe the line."

I gulped and hurriedly tidied my workstation. "I'm only following Lord Rupert's instructions."

Chef Heston glowered at me for several seconds before sighing. "Very well. I can make his favorite dinner. Don't mess up the cakes."

I opened my mouth to protest. I never messed up the cakes. Then I thought better about challenging him. Chef Heston had been furious about the damaged bike when I'd gotten back to the castle that afternoon and had made me take it to the nearby repair store. I didn't need to give him another reason to be angry at me.

I put my head down, cleaned up, and then looked at the work schedule for tomorrow.

Audley Castle was popular all year round, with visitors arriving from all over the world to wonder at the stunning grounds and beautiful architecture.

Most days, we had several coachloads of tourists visiting the gardens and having a look around the rooms that were open to the public.

The Duke and Duchess still lived in the castle, along with their nephew, Lord Rupert, and their niece, Princess Alice, along with Lady Philippa Carnegie, the Duchess's mom. They opened certain rooms so visitors could delight in the architecture and priceless decor. Most rooms had velvet roped off areas so the expensive antiques couldn't be damaged. Room attendants walked around keeping an eye out for anyone foolish enough to jump over a rope to try to grab a selfie on a Louis the Fourteenth chaise lounge.

All those visitors always needed feeding. We had a large, popular café on site, and I was in the kitchen almost every day, baking and preparing treats.

The back door to the kitchen opened. Half a dozen mud-spattered gardeners trooped in, thumping their boots on the mat and rubbing their hands together.

"Get out!" Chef Heston roared, his face turning bright red as he glared at them.

I recognized Meredith Jones in the group. She was an assistant gardener and had joined the castle's large staff team at the same time as me.

She blinked rapidly at Chef Heston. "We're supposed to be here."

"This is my kitchen. I say who can come in." Chef Heston stomped over to the group and pointed a finger at the door. "Out! You're all filthy."

"Princess Alice sent us in for tea," Meredith said. "She said it would be fine."

"That's right," another gardener, Jacob, said. "She told us we'd all worked so hard today that we deserved a treat."

"Not in my kitchen," Chef Heston growled out. "I won't have mud stamped around my pristine working environment. Outside, all of you, now."

I bit my bottom lip to stop from chuckling. It was so typical of Princess Alice. She was such a sweet person and was always looking out for the members of staff who helped keep Audley Castle running so smoothly. She wouldn't have thought twice about suggesting the gardeners come inside and make themselves hot drinks and get some food.

The group of gardeners glowered at Chef Heston before turning and stomping out the door.

"Unbelievable!" he said as the door slammed behind the last one. "That'll need to be cleared up." He hurried out of the kitchen, yelling at Louise Atkins, our fabulous new junior sous chef, to grab a broom.

She rolled her eyes at me as she dashed to the cleaning closet. "He's such a jerk."

I nodded. "He's determined not to lose his five stars for hygiene."

"Then he should clean up the mud." Louise grabbed a broom and made swift work of making it look like the gardeners had never been there.

I waited until Chef Heston had gone to the supply store before hurriedly heaping a pile of iced fairy cakes and miniature Battenberg cakes on a tray and walking out after the gardeners.

They were only a short distance away, packing their tools into the back of their cars and vans. Several of the team were volunteers and brought their own equipment with them.

They did amazing things with the gardens, including providing some herbs I used in my cooking. I wanted to stay on their good side.

"Wait up!" I hurried over with the cakes.

They all gathered around, hungrily eyeing the treats.

"Help yourselves," I said. "Don't worry about Chef Heston. He's been in a bad mood all day."

Meredith nodded a thanks as she took a cake. "Isn't that his default setting? Every time I see him, he's yelling at somebody."

"It's how he likes to keep order. Although I'm beginning to figure out his bark is a lot worse than his bite, but I still try to keep out of his way."

"Good idea," she said. "This is delicious. Did you make these fairy cakes?"

I smiled. "Yes, it's my own recipe. Elderflower and orange with an orange zest buttercream."

"You're a genius in the kitchen," Meredith said. "Thanks so much."

The other gardeners also said thanks as they hurriedly polished off the tray of cakes. Working long hours in the grounds definitely worked up an appetite.

I lifted my head as two cars rumbled across the gravel driveway to the door used exclusively by members of the household. A Porsche and a Ferrari slid to a stop.

That must be Rupert's friends arriving for their old school get-together. "I'd better go. I'm catering for a party tonight." I waved goodbye to the gardeners and hurried back to the kitchen to finish up my desserts.

I'd planned three different desserts for this evening, all Rupert's favorites. Mini fresh cream and berry pavlovas, tiny Italian lemon glazed tarts with a fresh lemon drizzle, and triple chocolate brownie bites with a warm ganache filling.

With the treats laid out in front of me, I picked up the bag of icing and set to work on the decorations for the brownies. I loved to add little finishing touches and flourishes to show it was my own work. Nothing over the top, not lots of glitter or stick on edible decorations, just delicate flowers or little swirls of lemon zest to finish things off. It was the tiny touches that made my cakes stand out.

I was icing the last row of brownies when the kitchen door opened. Rupert hurried in, fiddling with the gray silk cravat he wore.

"I won't be long with the desserts," I said.

He nodded, his gaze flickering around the kitchen. "Jolly good. I'm looking forward to them."

"Is everything okay?" I lowered the icing bag. I could feel the nerves radiating off Rupert as he strode around the kitchen.

"Oh, it's nothing. It's just that, well, I want to make a good impression."

"I'm sure you will. They're your friends. You don't need to impress them. They already like you."

His smile was rueful. "Well, it's the old school network, you see. I wouldn't say they're my best friends, but we grew up together. There's always a bit of one-upmanship at these events. We take it in turns to hold them. Last year, Kendal hired this enormous yacht and took us out for the day. I was horribly seasick and everyone laughed at me."

My forehead wrinkled, not liking that idea one bit. "They're not very good friends if they don't take care of you when you're not well."

He shrugged as he continued to fiddle with his cravat.

"How's your head after our little ... encounter?" I asked.

"Campbell was worrying about nothing. I'm fine. Just a little lump, that's all. And are you sure you're okay? I didn't like to abandon you, but Campbell can be very persuasive."

"I'm just perfect," I said. "It takes a lot to stop me from baking."

A smile lit his face as his blue eyes sparkled. Rupert was classically handsome with a wide mouth and perfect teeth. "Which is good news. And those look delicious."

"You can have one if you like. You need to make sure they're good enough for your friends."

"I trust you, Holly." He glanced at the door and his hands twisted together. He paced around, inspected the knives on the chopping board, and then walked to the back door.

I needed to distract him. His anxiety was making me sweat. "Would you like to ice a brownie?" I asked.

Rupert turned and stared at me. "Oh! I'm not good at that kind of thing. Not very dexterous." He wiggled his fingers in the air.

"I've heard you playing the piano. You must be dexterous to be able to do that so well."

"You've heard me?"

My cheeks flushed with heat. "Well, not intentionally, but I was passing the music room and heard something lovely. When I peeked inside, you were playing. You're very talented."

"It takes many hours of practice and a tyrant of a teacher to become that talented." His own cheeks glowed. "But thank you for the compliment."

"You should try icing. It's fun. I can show you."

After a second of hesitation, he walked over and looked at the brownies. "I don't want to destroy your beautiful creations."

"If it doesn't work out, you can always hide the evidence easily enough." I patted my stomach.

"Aha! Yes, very good. Excellent plan. Very well. Let's have a go. What do I need to do?"

I handed him the icing bag. "Keep the top twisted so the icing doesn't squeeze out. Aim the nozzle at the center of the brownie and push down slowly."

Rupert shuffled his feet as he got into position and grasped the icing bag. "Like this?"

"Move your hand a little lower down the bag." I gently adjusted his hand. "And now, all you need to do is squeeze."

Nothing happened for a few seconds. Then a huge blob of chocolate icing shot out and landed with a splat on the counter.

"Oh! This is trickier than it looks." He held the icing bag away from him.

"Try again. Let me guide you." I placed my hand over his and aimed the nozzle. "Squeeze very gently. If you press too hard, the icing bag can explode."

Rupert chuckled and cleared his throat. "You're so good at this, Holly. A real professional."

I glanced up and noticed how flushed his cheeks still were. I instantly stepped back. Lord Rupert was a good-looking guy and had a voice that could charm angels, but he was nobility. And I was, well, I was awesome in my own way, but definitely not meant for tiaras and ball gowns.

"Maybe you're right." I extracted the icing bag from his hands. "I'll stick to the icing."

"And I'll stick to …" His brow wrinkled. "Well, I'm not actually sure what I'm any good at."

"You're good at lots of things. Your music for one. And you love gardening." Rupert was always out with the team of gardeners.

His mouth twisted to the side. "I may love gardening, but gardens don't love me. I've been trying to cultivate that herb garden for six months. Everything dies. I think I have black fingers, not green fingers."

"You enjoy it. That's the main thing."

He jabbed a finger at me. "You're right. And you can only get better with practice. I learned that from my terrifying piano teacher."

"Absolutely! You should have seen the first few cakes I made. Burned on the bottom and soggy in the middle. They were inedible."

He laughed. "I really can't imagine that. Everything you make tastes like magic."

"You've yet to sample my attempt at Roman honey bread," I said. "I can't get it right."

"I'm sure it will be delicious. I'll have several slices when you're ready to showcase it."

"Let me perfect the recipe first before I let it loose on you. I don't want Campbell accusing me of poisoning you as well as trying to run you over with my bike."

"Oh dear, don't mind him. He's terribly protective of us all."

"Which is a good thing. That's his job."

He chuckled. "Right again, Holly. Not only an amazing cook and pretty, but clever too. You really are the whole package."

I grabbed a cloth and flapped it. "That's kind of you to say."

Rupert cleared his throat as an awkward silence grew between us. "Oh! Before I forget, Granny's requested your presence."

My heart jumped. "She has?"

"Yes! She wants extra dessert. When I told her about this evening and the food, she insisted on sampling the treats you've made."

"Perhaps you could take them to her." I gestured at the cakes. "I've still got a lot to do here."

"I would, but she insisted on you. I think she rather likes you. Well, I'd better get on. My guests are settling in, and they'll be wondering what happened to me." Rupert nodded, smoothed a hand over his messy hair that always looked in need of a good brush, and hurried out of the kitchen.

The door shut behind him, and I took a deep breath. Oh boy. Lady Philippa Carnegie wanted to see me. I liked the old lady, but she was as eccentric as they came.

And if that wasn't unsettling enough, the east turret where she lived was rumored to be haunted.

Chapter 4

Half an hour later, I ran my gaze over the desserts. They were ready to go. I'd placed the trays in the cooler cabinet until it was time to take them to Lord Rupert and his guests.

I selected a small china plate from the cabinet in the kitchen and placed three small cakes on it, choosing one of each so Lady Philippa had a good selection.

I'd been to visit her a dozen times in her private quarters in the east turret of the castle. Every time I went for a visit, I got the chills.

There were rumors and legends about the east turret. Not least of which included several ghosts who put in an appearance and scared people.

I'd yet to see them, and hoped I never would, but I'd experienced a fair few cold spots. Apparently, that meant a ghost was lurking around.

I wasn't making this journey on my own, though. Chef Heston refused to let Meatball in the kitchen while I was at work, which was fair enough. No one liked free fur in their food. Instead, he got to spend his days in a luxurious kennel right outside the kitchen door.

I'd paid to have it installed, after getting permission from Duchess Audley. She was a huge dog lover, and the owner of six feisty, pampered corgis, and had been only too pleased to accommodate Meatball.

I poked my head out the back door and whistled softly.

Meatball's head appeared from the kennel before he hopped up and hurried toward me, his little tail wagging with delight.

"How would you like to go see Lady Philippa? She loves you."

"Woof woof." The tail wagged harder. She always had a treat ready for Meatball when we visited.

"And you can see Horatio," I said.

The tail stopped wagging. "Woof."

"Be nice to Horatio. He's an old dog. That means he can be grumpy."

"Woof woof."

"And he's a royal dog, so we need to be on our best behavior around him." Horatio was an ancient, gassy, mildly overweight corgi who enjoyed nothing more than snoring loudly on the stunning four poster bed in Lady Philippa's bedroom. When he was awake, he spent the whole time glaring at Meatball and growling if he got too close. Poor Meatball. He only wanted to make friends, but Horatio was having none of it.

I checked the coast was clear, and Chef Heston wasn't around, before hurrying through the kitchen with Meatball. I grabbed the cakes, and we dashed into the corridor. It led to a large open-plan hallway, lined with dark polished wood furniture. Framed portraits of members of the Audley family lined the walls as we hurried to the stairs of the east wing turret.

The stairs were made of stone and twisted around as they led up to Lady Philippa's private quarters.

It was one hundred and fifty-two steps to the top. I'd counted them the first time I'd come up here.

I slowed as we reached step thirty. Every time I passed this spot, there was an intense cold draft. I swallowed. It wasn't a ghost. Nothing spectral was about to fly out and scare me.

Meatball tilted his head and his ears lowered. He barked three times.

"It's just a cold draft. There's probably a gap in the stone." I raced past the cold spot to be on the safe side. There was no point in tempting fate.

We'd made it halfway up the stairs when there was a loud thud behind me. I increased my pace, my heart racing.

"There is no such thing as ghosts. There is no such thing as ghosts," I whispered repeatedly. "It's just an old spooky turret. There's nothing to see here."

Meatball was as jumpy as me and scrambled up the stairs as fast as his stubby legs would let him, his nose bumping into my ankle in his haste to get away from the cold and the strange noises.

I slowed as I peered out of a narrow window. They'd been designed for use by archers who'd protected the castle from potential invaders hundreds of years ago.

Meatball pushed past me and bounced on his paws as he waited at the top of the steps, the fur on his back standing up. He knew the perilous journey was worth it. Lady Philippa only had the best food in for Horatio, and she always shared his treats when Meatball came calling.

I blew out a breath, my thigh muscles aching from the steep climb as I reached the final step. We'd made it in one piece.

We reached a closed wooden door that led into the corridor of Lady Philippa's private quarters. Well, I called them private quarters. She called it her own private prison.

I was about to push the door open, when it creaked on its hinges and slowly opened on its own.

Meatball took a step back and whimpered.

I rested a hand over my heart and peered cautiously around the door, half expecting to see a ghost behind it. Of course, there was nothing there.

"It was just a breeze," I said quietly. I shuffled around the door, Meatball glued to my heels.

The corridor was made of stone and had large leaded windows set along one wall. The windows looked over some of the beautiful gardens of Audley Castle, displaying a stunning ornate rose garden, which Lady Philippa loved to look at.

"Who's there?" a high-pitched voice called out.

"It's Holly Holmes, Lady Philippa." I hurried to the end of the corridor to another door which stood ajar and pulled it open.

"Holly! Of course, I asked Rupert to send you. I hope you've brought me plenty of treats."

I smiled at her as I walked in. Lady Philippa was a well-preserved seventy-eight, with beautiful high cheekbones and porcelain skin that was only faintly lined. She had a neat blunt bob that was currently dyed a startling magenta. She was dressed head to toe in pale pink silk and had three rows of pearls around her neck.

She gestured me in with a glittering, ring covered hand. "Don't stand on ceremony, girl. You're always welcome in here."

A loud snort came from Lady Philippa's bedroom. That must be Horatio, no doubt resting his pampered furry head on a silk pillow.

"Where would you like your cake?" I asked Lady Philippa.

"On the table beside me is fine." She patted the seat next to her. "And you must join me. I haven't seen anyone all day. No one wants to talk to an old woman these days."

"That's very kind of you, but I'm catering a party for Lord Rupert this evening."

Lady Philippa sighed and her gaze dropped. "I get so lonely stuck in this tower. My daughter is cruel for keeping me locked in here."

I bit my bottom lip. Every time I saw Lady Philippa, she mentioned how she'd been banished to the turret. The problem with that was the door was open. She could walk down the stairs any time she liked.

I could spare her ten minutes. I settled in the seat. "You should arrange a trip out one day."

She turned and smiled at me. "Oh, no. It wouldn't be approved of. Isabella always says I cause problems wherever I go. It's why she keeps me trapped here. I'm a prisoner in my own home."

"Just a walk around the gardens might be nice."

Lady Philippa selected a lemon tart as she waved a hand in the air. "Enough glum talk. How's your love life?"

I sucked in a breath. Here was a woman who got straight to the important stuff. "Well, I mean, work keeps me busy. And I'm not really looking for anybody."

"You should always be looking for someone, my dear. My marriage to William was such a happy one. He swept me off my feet with his grand gestures. Have I told you, he used to send me a bouquet of flowers every day until I agreed to marry him? Two hundred and seventeen bouquets. That's commitment."

I smiled and nodded. Lady Philippa loved to talk about her late husband, William Carnegie.

"And he would write me poems. I never liked to tell him that they weren't particularly good, but it was such a sweet gesture. Rupert enjoys poetry too. He must have gotten his love of that from William. He often read to him when he was a child."

"I've heard Lord Rupert reciting poetry," I said. "He does enjoy it."

Her blue eyes narrowed a fraction. "He's a good boy. Single too, in case you haven't noticed."

"Um, well, he must be waiting for the right person." Lady Philippa couldn't seriously be thinking about matchmaking us.

"And he comes to see me regularly. I barely see Isabella these days. I can't remember the last time she came for a visit."

"Wasn't she here two days ago? I remember her ordering afternoon tea from the kitchen for you."

"Oh, no. You must be mistaken." She nibbled the edge off the tart.

I got the impression that Lady Philippa enjoyed the drama that came with living in a turret. It was like some grand romantic tragedy where the heroine was trapped and kept from enjoying her freedom. The truth was, she'd shared over fifty happy years with William before he'd died in his sleep. That was a lot more happiness than most people got, and her family was always coming to see her.

"You need to find yourself a nice young man," she said.

"I'm still finding my feet in the castle. I've only been here a few months. There's still a lot to learn. I've no time for romance."

"There's nothing you need to learn when it comes to baking. Your cakes are divine." She smiled warmly. "I'm so glad we found you. Although it was a pity your café had to close."

"You knew about my café?"

"Of course. I keep an eye on everything that happens in the village. We are caretakers of this wonderful place. I even had my chauffeur place an order on my behalf once or twice. I wasn't disappointed. And when I learned you were joining the staff, I was delighted that I'd have access to your cakes at all times."

"I do miss my café," I said. "But I enjoy working here."

"I wonder if you might make me those—" Lady Philippa tensed in her seat. The tart she held dropped onto her silks as she grabbed a notepad off the table and began to scribble with a pen.

"Is something the matter?" I leaned forward in my seat as she continued to scribble rapidly across the page.

Her cheeks were pale as she sucked in a shuddering breath. "Death is coming to Audley."

I jerked back in my seat. "What do you mean?" I'd heard so many things about Lady Philippa. Some people claimed she could see the future. Others said she had the ability to curse people who did her wrong. I didn't believe any of that, but her current behavior was certainly odd.

Her hand flew to her mouth. "Oh my! It involves Rupert."

"Lord Rupert's going to die? What should we do? Should I tell him? We can increase the security presence around him. I can call the police. How about—"

"No! He's not the one who will die, but death is following him like a second shadow." Lady Philippa's hand shook as she lowered it into her lap. "Holly, you must protect him for me."

I tilted my head as my brow lowered. "I … um, well, he's got a great security team around him. I'm sure they'll spot if there's any danger."

"You understand him. He trusts you. If you tell him he's in danger, he'll listen. I know what that boy is like. He always has his head in the clouds. He never sees a problem until it's too late."

My thoughts turned to the recent incident with the bike. Rupert really hadn't spotted me. Maybe he did need somebody else looking out for him if danger was coming his way.

Lady Philippa reached over and grabbed my hand. "You must protect him. Guard him with your life. He's such a precious boy. I cannot imagine a world where Rupert isn't in it."

I patted her hand. "I'll keep an eye on him. I'm sure there's nothing to worry about, though. He's spending a long weekend with his best friends. No harm will come to him."

"I see the truth. Rupert's in trouble. I cannot be there myself to protect him given my current incarceration."

I glanced at the open door. "Lady Philippa, you do realize you can leave any time you like?"

She lifted a finger to her lips, and her gaze darted around the room. "Don't be fooled. The door may well be open, but it doesn't mean I can walk through it."

I glanced at the door again, not at all certain what that meant. "If it makes you feel any better, of course I'll look out for Lord Rupert."

A relieved sigh shot out of her mouth. "Thank you so much."

"May I?" I gestured to the fallen tart staining her beautiful silks.

"Oh! I'd forgotten all about the food." She nodded at me.

I scooped the tart into a napkin.

Meatball whined and nudged the tart with his nose.

"Where are my manners?" Lady Philippa seemed to forget about her startling revelation about murder as she pulled three dog treats from her jacket pocket.

Meatball stood on his hind legs and waggled his front paws in the air.

She laughed as she tossed him the treats. "He's such a delightful dog."

"I happen to agree." Meatball was one of a kind, and I wouldn't have him any other way.

"I'm so glad to have you here." Lady Philippa reached up and unclipped the pearls from around her neck. "Have these as payment for taking care of Rupert."

I shook my head. Those pearls were worth a fortune. "No! There's absolutely no need to pay me. I could never take your pearls."

She ran the pearls through her fingers. "They belonged to my great-great-grandmother. She was a terrible woman. She always liked to find fault in people. It would be amusing to give them to you. You could wear them in the kitchen while you worked. She'd spin in her grave. Hah! I should insist you take them simply because of that."

"I'm certain Chef Heston would have something to say about me wearing pearls while I worked. If one fell in the food, it would be a choking hazard. Please, Lady Philippa, keep your pearls. I'm happy to keep an eye on Lord Rupert. I don't want to see him getting in any trouble. Although I can't imagine what danger's coming his way."

Her nose wrinkled. "When I have a hunch like this, I never ignore it. Bad things always happen if I don't pay attention." Lady Philippa's gaze drifted to the window.

I took the opportunity to take a peek at the open notepad she'd scribbled in. My stomach clenched. Even upside down, I could read some of the scribblings. The notebook was full of dark portents and predictions of bad things happening to members of the family.

Just how accurate could they be? And what was I getting myself into by agreeing to keep Lord Rupert safe?

Chapter 5

After sitting with Lady Philippa for a few more minutes, I needed to get back to the kitchen.

Her thoughts were definitely elsewhere, and she barely noticed me as I left the turret with Meatball and hurried back down the stone staircase, making sure I dashed past the cold spots without stopping to inspect them.

I shouldn't dwell on Lady Philippa's unsettling prediction about a death. Maybe she saw things from her turret that other people missed. She had a pair of high-powered binoculars perched on a window ledge that she used to watch the goings on in the grounds. Could she have spooked herself by staring at too many shadows? Maybe the castle ghost rumors were getting to her too.

Lady Philippa wasn't conjuring up curses or making bad things happen to people. That was impossible, wasn't it?

After putting Meatball in his kennel with the promise of a delicious supper once I was finished for the evening, I neatly laid out the desserts I'd prepared.

There was no one else in the kitchen while I worked, which was unusual. There was usually some sort of activity going on. It was either preparation for the next day or people hurrying around getting the family's evening meal ready. Then I remembered, it was games night.

All the staff got together for an evening off once a week, all thanks to the Duchess. It was a long-held tradition in the castle going back hundreds of years. There were tables laid out with different games in one of the parlors. Some were card games, others board games. It was a fun way for the staff to relax after the often hectic and busy activities of the day.

And once a year, the castle residents even served the staff. It was a complete role reversal, as the Duchess and her family provided the food and served the drinks, but that wasn't happening for months.

I didn't feel like joining in games night. I wanted a quiet night with just me and Meatball, especially after the shock revelation from Lady Philippa about death coming to the castle.

Given the lack of serving staff around, I had no choice but to set the desserts on a trolley, along with plates, napkins, and cutlery, and walk into the main castle to discover where Rupert and his friends were.

It didn't take many minutes before I heard raucous laughter coming from the games room. I knocked on the door and waited.

It was opened a few seconds later. Rupert smiled broadly, his cheeks flushed as he stood there with a glass of whiskey in his hand.

"Holly! Of course, it's dessert time. Do come in." He stood back, and I walked into the room.

There were four men in there, along with Rupert, all around his age. They exuded the kind of confident aura that came with an expensive education and a moneyed background.

"Set the desserts on the table," Rupert said. "Everyone, I've been telling you all about Holly's wonderful desserts.

It looks like she's surpassed herself this evening. She's an absolute wizard in the kitchen."

I flushed under his praise as I pushed the trolley in and laid everything out.

"That looks delicious." A tall lean man with dark floppy hair strode over and winked at me. "Rupert forgot to mention how sweet you appear to be as well."

A startled laugh shot out of Rupert. "Steady on. Holly's here to work."

"And I bet she obeys all your orders." The man stepped closer.

"That's enough, Kendal. Leave the woman alone." A shorter, broad-shouldered man with dark hair and stubble shook his head as he approached and looked at the desserts. "Ignore him. He has no manners when he sees something he wants."

I forced a smile as Kendal did his best to invade my personal space. I resisted the urge to stamp on his foot and tell him to back off as I passed him a plate.

Rupert cleared his throat. "Holly, this is Kendal Jakes and Christian Knightsbridge. We went to school together and even shared the same dorm. It was great fun."

"It wasn't all that great." Another guy joined them and selected a brownie. He had sandy brown hair and brilliant green eyes. "We had to listen to Tony's snoring for the whole year."

The only man not to join us as he lounged in a leather armchair chuckled loudly. "I do not snore."

"You absolutely do," the guy with the sandy hair said.

Rupert nodded. "I'm afraid you do, Tony." He smiled at me. "And this is Simon Napleton. He was head of our school house. The chap sitting down is Anthony Bambridge."

Simon nodded as he ate one of my cakes. "This sure beats the food we were served at Eton."

"I'm glad you like it." I took a step back, eager to return to the sanctuary of the kitchen and away from Kendal's lecherous glances.

"Don't leave so soon." Kendal caught hold of my arm. "We've yet to sample your delights."

"Haven't you got enough on your plate?" Christian threw a muscular arm around Kendal's shoulder.

Kendal glared at him and dropped his hold on my arm. "I don't know what you mean."

"The last I heard, you had a married woman on the go and were seeing Izzie Northcott. You don't want to take on the kitchen assistant as well."

"Holly's not a kitchen assistant," Rupert said swiftly. "She's a skilled baker. We're lucky to have her."

"Yeah?" Kendal looked at him and smirked. "Just how lucky have you gotten with her?"

My lips pursed, and I took a step back. "If you'll excuse me. I have work to do."

"Don't go." Kendal placed a hand over his heart. "I miss you already."

Rupert's gaze was apologetic as he hurried to the door with me. "I'm so sorry about that. They've all had a bit to drink. I promise you, their manners aren't usually this bad."

I shook my head. It wasn't the first time I'd encountered men of privilege who thought they were entitled to everything they took a liking to. "I'm happy to provide you with the desserts, but that's all."

His cheeks grew bright pink, and he stuttered out several half words. "Oh! Of course. The thought never entered my head. I didn't bring you here for … that. I mean, not that you aren't attractive. I've always admired your dark eyes. You're very beautiful. Any man would be lucky to have you. I mean … oh dear, I think I may have had too much to drink as well. Sorry. I should stick to the soft stuff."

I accepted his bumbled apology with a nod. "Really, it's not a problem. Enjoy the rest of your evening." I slid out the door and closed it behind me before letting out a sigh. Rupert thought I was beautiful. That shouldn't make me smile, but it did.

I spotted Duke Henry Audley and Duchess Isabella Audley walking toward me.

The Duke and Duchess were Rupert and Alice's aunt and uncle. Their father, George Audley, had left them in their care while he traveled. A journey which had taken almost twenty years to complete and was still ongoing according to the village gossip.

I wasn't surprised to see them this time of the evening. They stayed in their private quarters during the day when the tourists were wandering about, but it wasn't unusual to find them taking a stroll around the castle in the evening.

Duke Audley was a tall, imposing man with dark hair shot through with gray. He had a long regal nose and intelligent blue eyes. Sadly, his actual intelligence had gone missing somewhere along the way. He'd often talk as if we still lived in Victorian times when staff were nothing more than glorified slaves at the beck and call of their master.

Fortunately, Duchess Isabella Audley had her head screwed on the right way and was the real power in this household. She was possibly one of the most beautiful women I'd ever seen. She was tall and elegant and seemed to glide as she walked. She had porcelain skin and large blue eyes that always held interest and warmth whenever she spoke.

"Good evening, Holly." Duchess Isabella smiled at me. "You're working late tonight."

Before I got the chance to reply, the air was filled with frantic yapping. Four plump corgis bounded up to the Duke and Duchess.

Duchess Isabella loved her dogs, so I'd known right away we'd get along. Unfortunately, the castle corgis were spoiled, overindulged brats who bullied Meatball whenever they saw him. Don't get me wrong, he held his own, but four against one would never be a fair fight.

The corgis came to a stop by the Duchess's heel, guarding her as if she were at risk by talking to a servant. Their beady eyes fixed on me, waiting for me to make a wrong move.

"I'm just providing the desserts for Lord Rupert's evening with his friends," I said.

"Ah! Of course. I'd forgotten he'd invited them for a few days. Does it appear to be going well?" she asked.

"Of course it will be going well," Duke Audley said in his usual thin, distracted sounding voice. "Our nephew knows how to entertain."

The Duchess patted his arm. "Of course. Although I recall him having a tough time with those boys when they were at Eton."

"Stuff and nonsense," the Duke said. "Rupert can make friends with anybody. And everyone will want to be his friend, given his position."

"Which isn't always a good thing." The Duchess smiled indulgently at her husband as he drifted off to look at an oil painting on the wall. "I probably shouldn't say this, but Rupert had a difficult time when he was younger. He's such a sensitive soul. He feels very deeply, and that's a difficult thing for a teenage boy, especially when he's surrounded by other boys. I often worried that he might have been bullied at school."

My mouth twisted to the side. Sadly, I could imagine that happening. He did have a gentle manner. Rupert genuinely cared about other people's well-being. It was a rare trait.

"Was this my great-grandfather?" the Duke asked.

"No, my sweet. That was the Lord Chancellor. He was your second cousin." She discreetly shook her head. "There are so many portraits of friends and relatives littered around the castle, it's difficult to remember who everyone is." She patted my arm. "How's everything in the kitchens? Making more delicious treats to spoil us with?"

"We're keeping busy," I said. "I'm working on perfecting an old recipe I found. I thought it might be nice to serve some traditional food in the café."

"Traditional food?" Her nose wrinkled. "I fear traditional British food isn't up to much. It makes me think of lumpy oatmeal and overcooked vegetables."

I chuckled. "Well, technically, this is an import. It's a recipe for Roman honey bread. The problem is, I've tried several variations of recipes and nothing works. I feel like I'm missing something vital."

"If you wish to use our private library to conduct your research you're very welcome," the Duchess said. "We have a wide catalog of recipe books. They simply sit there gathering dust. It would be wonderful if somebody made use of them."

"I'd love that. Only if it's not an inconvenience to you." The castle library contained over three thousand books, many of them rare and valuable.

"Of course not." She smiled again. "And if I get to sample the finished product, I would be more than happy. You may consider that your payment for using our library."

"It's a deal. I'll happily make you as many Roman honey breads as you desire."

"And this chap is the …" The Duke stared at another picture.

"I'd better go," the Duchess said, "before my lovely husband forgets his own name." She hurried away, accompanied by the yapping corgis.

Her words about Rupert being bullied stayed with me as I walked back to the kitchen. He was a kind man. He deserved so much better than that. I hoped his friends weren't being mean to him this evening.

I shook my head. I shouldn't be thinking about Rupert in that way. Baking was my one true love. And, of course, Meatball. As I'd said to Lady Philippa, I had no room in my life for a relationship. Even though I occasionally felt a little lonely.

Thinking about Meatball, I was overdue giving him the supper I'd promised him.

I slowed as a movement in the main courtyard caught my eye. There was a flash of something pale that vanished the second I stepped closer to take a look.

I rubbed my arms as a shudder ran down my spine. It was nothing. It didn't have anything to do with Lady Philippa's prediction about trouble for Rupert. There were no mysterious figures lurking outside. And even if there were, the security team sweeping the grounds would pick them up. Campbell would make sure of it.

I had nothing to worry about. This was real life, not some spooky murder mystery.

Chapter 6

I swiped my hand across my forehead and let out an exhausted sigh. It was the end of another long day of cake deliveries and baking, and after yesterday being so busy, I was more than ready for a hot bath and an early night.

Meatball had other ideas. He bounced by the back door of the kitchen as I sat at the table, sipping on a welcome mug of tea.

Given how small he was, you'd think he didn't need long walks, but I had a feeling he was crossed with something like a terrier. That gave him boundless amounts of energy, and he loved nothing more than romping around for hours outside.

"Are you sure you don't want to put your paws up and have an early night?" I asked.

"Woof." That was a definite doggy no. He continued to bounce by the door, leaping up in the hope he'd be able to open it for himself if he could just get high enough.

I had to keep a lookout for Chef Heston. Most of the staff had clocked off for the evening, but he was prowling around somewhere. If he realized I'd snuck Meatball in the kitchen while I had a five-minute break, he'd go mad.

Meatball knew his place though and stayed on the mat by the back door. He'd heard Chef Heston yell at people one too many times to know he didn't want to get in his way.

"Woof woof." Meatball pawed at the door.

My gaze went to the window. The sun was just dipping below the tree line. A pale peach bloom filtered across a gentle layer of thin white cloud.

"Okay, we can go for a walk." I finished my tea, placed the mug in the dishwasher, and headed outside.

I took Meatball's leash with me, although he rarely needed it when we were in the grounds. I only used it when he was in the bicycle basket to make sure he was safely attached. And he was well-behaved, always returning when I called him. Well, he returned nine times out of ten. I called that a win.

We wandered around the side of the castle, passing the ornate rose garden full of fragrant blooms, and walked past the dozens of clipped hedgerows shaped into beautiful patterns of diamonds, circles, and arches.

I stopped and tilted my head. High-pitched yapping sounded nearby. I grimaced. "Meatball! This way." We headed in the opposite direction. I didn't want to run into the castle's evil corgis this evening. Meatball did enjoy a good dustup with those spoiled dogs, but he didn't always come out on top when they ganged up on him in a furry, spiteful pack.

Meatball raced ahead, his ears up and his little legs flying. He disappeared around the corner, and I ambled after him, not in any hurry. My leg muscles ached from all the cycling I'd done today. A gentle walk was about all I could manage.

"Woof woof." From the higher pitch of Meatball's bark, he'd found something or someone he was happy about.

Two more barks came, followed by a high-pitched giggle.

I smiled as I recognized that laugh. I turned the corner and shook my head as Princess Alice scooped Meatball into her arms and hugged him.

"He might have muddy paws." I strolled toward them.

Princess Alice wore a beautiful long white dress that would no longer be pristine thanks to Meatball's enthusiastic squirming as he tried to lick her heart-shaped face.

"Don't worry about this old thing." She kissed Meatball on the head several times before placing him back on the ground, where he bounced around her ankles with delight. "I always have to cuddle this adorable fluffy beast whenever we meet."

Alice had inherited the family traits of blonde hair, which she wore down to her waist, and sparkling blue eyes. She was curvier than Duchess Isabella, thanks to her love of sneaking into the kitchen and sampling the treats we put out for the castle customers.

"What are you doing out here?" I asked.

She gestured to the easel behind her. "Getting in some drawing practice. Mommy says I have to be an accomplished woman in the arts. Drawing, painting, needlepoint, music, and singing. And don't get me started on the dancing. We've got a whole summer of balls ahead of us and I still haven't mastered the foxtrot. My instructor told me I have two left feet."

I glanced over her shoulder at the easel. There were several crooked looking blue flowers and what might be a large black stick on the paper.

Alice groaned. "I know, isn't it terrible? Some people don't have an artistic eye. I'm always telling Mommy that. She never listens. Drawing is so yawnsville. What's the point in it?"

I smiled as Alice continued to extol all the reasons why she shouldn't learn to draw.

We'd met during my first week working at the castle. I'd literally bumped into her and narrowly avoided throwing a large chocolate cake on her head. At first, I hadn't recognized her. She'd been dressed in dungarees and a baseball cap and had been sneaking in through the kitchen to avoid being spotted.

She'd sworn me to secrecy after I figured out who she was and confessed she'd been hiding in an empty staff apartment because she didn't want to go away on an etiquette weekend retreat. Alice had pretended she'd gone and didn't want anyone to know the truth.

I saw no harm in keeping her secret. Since then, she'd considered me a friend.

"Can you draw?" she asked. "Maybe you can do my flowers for me. I had a friend in school who always did my artwork. She was an absolute ace. She could draw anything. I'm more stick figure than Salvador Dali."

"I was never that good at art either," I said.

"Your cakes are works of art. I consider that a purposeful art. At least you can eat what you make."

"That's true," I said.

"I've been meaning to catch up with you. I found a new member of our family." Alice was obsessed with charting her family's ancient history.

"Who is it this time? Pirate, infamous soldier, or a wealthy baron?"

"A wool trader." She clamped a hand over her mouth and giggled. "Can you believe it? We're descended from trade. Apparently, he grew wealthy exporting wool to other countries. He was the one who bought the land the castle now stands on. There was an old monastery on the site which he tore down and began the foundations of Audley Castle. Although back then, it was a manor house. Nothing on this scale. Still, we are no better than you. Oh! That's a terrible thing to say. I mean, you're lovely. I'd love to be as good as you in the kitchen. But, well, you understand. Don't hate me."

I suppressed a smile. "I could never hate you. Everyone has to start somewhere."

"Exactly! I've got plenty more relatives to research before I'm finished, though. And I discovered some awful chap who had his head cut off. He was embezzling from the King. He got found out, thrown in the tower with his wife, and they lost their heads. Imagine that."

"That sounds terrifying. I'm glad you can't do that anymore."

"We jolly well can. Well, the Queen can. Someone commits treason against her, then it's off with their head."

Alice was naively sweet and as ditzy as they came. But as I'd gotten to know her over the last few months, I realized there was a brain inside that pretty head. She just liked to hide it.

"And I was thinking," she continued, "we could do a family tree for you."

"My family's small," I said. "My dad's no longer alive, and I know nothing about his family, other than that they came from Ireland."

"You've never mentioned your mom before," she said. "Where's she from?"

I sighed. That was a sensitive subject I rarely dug into. "My stepmom's lovely. She's vivacious and kind and really beautiful. She's always been there to help me."

"Your dad remarried after your birth mom left?"

"That's right. Mom just disappeared one day. Dad eventually got a divorce and settled down with Valerie. Even though dad's gone, I still stay in touch with her."

"And nobody else? You must have a larger family than that. Grandparents? Siblings? It can't just be you."

I shrugged. "I have a stepsister. Bianca can be a bit ... prickly. I don't think she ever warmed to the idea of her mom marrying my dad. I haven't heard from her in years. I also have a granny who's still alive. Granny Molly."

"What's she like?" Alice settled on the stool by her easel.

I rubbed the back of my neck. We didn't talk about Granny Molly. "She's ... unique." And serving five years in prison for fraud.

"That's a start. You know your parents' names and your granny's name. We can begin with that and work our way back. You may have a huge family dying to meet you. Wouldn't you like to know where you came from?"

I bit my lip. Given the criminal tendencies of some members of my family, and my mom's mysterious disappearance, I wasn't certain I did want to know. But my curiosity was piqued. I loved history and had even studied it at university. Although it hadn't led to a career in the subject, I'd always kept it as a hobby. I particularly loved the British Tudor period, with all the intrigue and scandal from the different members of the ruling elite.

"It could be fun to learn more," I said.

"Give me the details of your family and I'll set to work on it," Alice said.

"Shouldn't you concentrate on your drawing?"

She glared at the easel and poked her tongue out. "It's boring. I know I should be accomplished in every area, but why bother? Just because I know how to draw, it isn't going to bag me a fabulous man."

Alice had a sad past when it came to relationships. With two failed engagements behind her, she was considered something of a black sheep in the family. Her parents had written her off in terms of finding a suitable match. These days, they allowed her to do what she wanted, so long as she kept out of the limelight and didn't cause a scandal, especially not after breaking off her engagement to Lord Davenport.

Alice said that his flatulence had made her nauseous, and she couldn't imagine being with a man who made her so unwell. Unfortunately, that confession was made to a local reporter who'd delighted in printing it as a front-page story, getting the family plenty of national media attention.

"Woof woof." Meatball bounced around her feet.

"Quite right, beautiful boy. We need to take a walk together." Alice stood and tucked a hand through my elbow. "I hope my brother and his awful friends haven't been bothering you."

"Not really." I decided not to mention Kendal.

"They're just ghastly. So full of themselves. They think they're God's gift to women. Especially Kendal. He's such a disgusting letch. Watch out for him."

I couldn't disagree, especially considering how inappropriate he'd been around me. "Perhaps it's just high spirits."

"Bad manners more like. And they were out for hours clay pigeon shooting. It was so noisy! I was trying to take a nap and all I could hear was them popping those pointless bits of clay out of the sky."

I slowed and looked around the grounds. "They've finished shooting now?" Lady Philippa's premonition about a death prodded at me.

She giggled. "Of course they have, silly. Don't worry, no one's going to shoot us. I've no doubt they're stuffing their faces by now. They're so greedy. Besides, they weren't shooting around here. They were in the next field. We're perfectly safe."

We headed toward the trees in the grounds. Meatball always loved to explore in there. There were plenty of interesting smells and squirrels to chase.

He raced ahead and returned a few moments later, barking excitedly.

"What has he found?" Alice released her hold on my elbow.

"Probably a squirrel carcass."

Her nose crinkled. "Don't be gross. Wait right there, you cheeky boy."

"You shouldn't chase him." I shook my head as she hitched her dress up and disappeared from view, laughing loudly as she did so.

I strode after them. It was safe in the grounds, but it was dusk, and Alice had a habit of disappearing when she shouldn't.

I lost sight of them for several minutes before slowing as the sound of whining reached me. That was Meatball!

I increased my pace and hopped over a fallen log. "Meatball! Where are you?"

The whining increased, and he barked several times. Whatever he'd discovered, he didn't like it.

My heart pounded as I broke into a jog, looking around to try to spot either him or Alice.

He barked once again. Then several times one after the other. That was never a good sign. Multiple barks meant trouble was close by.

"Meatball!" I raced ahead, tripping over several roots and scraping my knee against a tree stump in my haste to find him.

"Oh! There you are." I ran into a small clearing.

Meatball stood with his front paws on Alice's back. She was flat out on the ground, not moving.

I raced over. "What happened?"

Meatball whined and backed up.

I turned Alice over. She was out cold, but I couldn't see that she'd hit her head or fallen. Had she fainted?

"Princess Alice." I checked her pulse, which was fine. What was going on here?

Meatball nudged me with his nose and barked several times.

"She's okay. We'll get her back to the castle as soon as she wakes. There's nothing to worry about." Even so, my heart was pounding too hard.

He nudged me again and scrabbled at the ground with his paws.

"What have you got there?" I leaned over Alice to the spot where Meatball was digging.

It took me a few seconds to process as my brain froze and my eyes refused to accept what I'd just seen.

There was no doubt about it though, no matter how many times I blinked. There was a hand poking out of the ground, and Meatball was digging it up.

Chapter 7

I jumped to my feet and staggered away from the rapidly deepening hole Meatball was digging around the hand.

No wonder Alice had fainted. I also felt lightheaded as I continued to stare at the gray, blotchy fingers.

My stomach clenched. What if it was somebody I knew?

I tried to remember the last time I'd seen Rupert. He hadn't stopped by the kitchen this morning, which was unusual. He'd often drop by for a tea and a chat.

I gulped. What if that was him in the ground?

Forcing my fear back to a manageable sense of chaos, I inched closer to the hand.

I blew out a breath. There was a silver pinkie ring on one finger and the nails were too neat to be Rupert's. He was a terrible nail biter and was always getting scolded by his sister for nibbling on his fingers.

Still, there was someone dead in the ground, and from the lack of a strong smell, they hadn't been there long.

I gently tugged Meatball away. "That's enough exploring. This must be a crime scene. If there's any evidence here, we need to make sure it isn't destroyed."

Meatball reluctantly relinquished his prize and came to stand beside me as I checked on Alice again.

"Wake up!" I shook her by the shoulder. I didn't want to deal with a body on my own.

She groaned and her eyes fluttered open. "What happened?"

"I think you fainted," I said.

She gasped. "Oh! The hand! I thought I saw a hand sticking out of the ground."

"You did. It's right over there." I pointed a few feet to our right.

She struggled to her knees and grabbed my arm as she looked around. "Is it … real?"

"I haven't touched it, but it looks real to me. And Meatball's very interested. He's got a keen sense of smell. This is just the sort of disgusting thing he'd find appealing. He once dug up a partially decaying toad from a swamp. He was so proud of himself."

"Woof woof." Meatball wagged his tail as if he knew exactly what I was talking about.

Princess Alice stared at the hand for several seconds before promptly keeling over and passing out again.

"No! I need your help." I looked back at the hand and shuddered. I didn't know what to do.

I left Alice on the ground and hurried a few steps away before turning and racing back. I had to get somebody else here. Call the police! I'd let them know what we'd discovered.

I'd just pulled my phone out of my back pocket when I froze. A branch had just snapped, the dry crunch sounding close.

My pulse raced and blood rushed to my head as adrenaline flooded through me. What if the killer was still here? We might have disturbed them as they covered the body. If they knew their victim had been discovered they might be back, thinking we'd seen them. They wouldn't risk anyone identifying them. We could be their next victims.

Stuffing my phone back in my pocket, I grabbed Alice under the armpits and dragged her behind a bush to a place of safety.

Meatball followed along closely, whining softly as if he sensed something was horribly wrong.

I pressed a finger to my lips to silence him. Maybe if we kept still and quiet, the killer wouldn't notice us.

There were more footsteps crunching through dried leaves. They were getting closer. It was too much of a risk hiding here. We were vulnerable.

I looked around and grabbed a large broken branch from the ground. That would do as a weapon.

Making sure Alice was carefully concealed, I sucked in a deep breath and stood, pressing my back against a tree trunk. I peeked out one side. There was nobody there.

I looked around the other side. I was certain I'd heard somebody. Maybe in my panicked state, I'd imagined it. After all, it wasn't every day you found a body buried in the woods. My mind was playing tricks on me, making me sensitive to potential danger.

Meatball nudged my leg with his nose and looked up at me.

I shook my head. I didn't want him getting involved. He might be a feisty dog, but he was only small, and he'd always rush to defend me if ever he thought I was in danger. There was no way I wanted him getting hurt.

I checked no one was around before ducking and racing to the next tree. The trunk was much broader, so it was easier for me to hide behind without being seen.

Meatball followed me, keeping his belly to the ground as if he sensed he needed to be discreet.

My mouth was dry and my hands clammy as more sounds filtered toward me. There was definitely at least one person out there. Maybe they were watching, waiting to see what my next move would be. Whatever they were planning, I wasn't going down without a fight.

The footsteps grew nearer. Any second now, they were going to come around the tree and see me. This might be the only chance I got to surprise them.

I tightened my grip on the branch, pulled back my arms as if I was holding a baseball bat ready to take a swing, stepped out from behind the tree, and let fly.

I was met with a startled grunt of surprise before a solid muscular arm slammed into my chest and knocked me flat on my back. The branch flew from my hand as the air was knocked from my lungs. My head bounced off the ground, which was fortunately cushioned by a carpet of dried leaves.

Even so, stars swam in my vision as I tried to get to my feet and confront my attacker. I flailed my arms wildly, wanting to make it as hard as possible to be grabbed.

Two firm hands pressed against my shoulders. Campbell Milligan's stern face came into view. "Holly Holmes! What are you doing out here?"

I gaped up at him. "It's you! You're the one sneaking about in the trees."

"*You're* the one sneaking." He glanced up, and I followed his gaze to the second security team member standing and watching silently. There was no expression on his grim face. I recognized Saracen, Campbell's right-hand man.

Campbell glared at me for another second before releasing his grip and holding out his hand.

I took it, and he almost yanked me off my feet as he lifted me.

I licked my lips and glanced from Campbell to Saracen. "I'm glad you're here. Although what are you doing here?"

"Princess Alice was seen entering the woods," Campbell said. "The Duchess doesn't like her walking alone. We were sent to find her. Where is she?"

"Oh, well, there's a bit of a story behind that." I cleared my throat and tried to gather my scattered thoughts. "She's okay, but she fainted."

Campbell removed the sunglasses he often wore and tucked them into a top pocket. His ice-blue eyes bored into me. "What did you do to make her faint?"

"Nothing! Her fainting has nothing to do with me."

He arched a brow and waited for me to continue.

There was no way I could sugar coat this. "Princess Alice fainted because she found a... a hand poking out of the ground."

A muscle twitched in Campbell's jaw. "Show me."

I hurried back to the clearing where the hand was still very visible. A wave of sickness ran through me, and I caught hold of a tree.

Campbell didn't appear to notice my distress. "Where's the princess?"

I gestured to the bush. "Behind there."

"Saracen, secure the princess. I'll check the area and make sure the scene hasn't been compromised too badly." He didn't even spare me a glance as he strode around the clearing.

Saracen headed to Princess Alice and kneeled over her, his fingers going to the pulse point in her neck.

"She's not hurt," I said as I hurried over. "She must have been surprised by what she discovered. Alice ran ahead of me when she was chasing Meatball and—"

Saracen glanced at me. "Meatball?"

"My dog." I gestured to him. He was standing by my side looking alert. "Anyway, Meatball ran ahead. He must have smelled the body. Princess Alice chased after him and

I lost them for a few minutes. When I found them, she was passed out and Meatball was digging up the body."

Saracen grunted.

"How's she doing?" I asked.

"Still unconscious," he said.

"She did wake up, but fainted again as soon as she remembered what she'd seen."

Saracen simply grunted again as he stood guard over Princess Alice.

Campbell emerged through the trees. "There's no sign of anyone else nearby. We need to make sure nobody else interferes with the crime scene and check for evidence. How's the princess?"

"No injuries," Saracen said.

"She's just in shock," I said.

Campbell glanced at me before striding over. "Try to wake her up."

Saracen nodded and knelt over Princess Alice again.

"Maybe I can help," I said. "She might be startled by your sudden arrival."

"Are you saying we're intimidating?" Campbell folded his arms across his broad chest.

"Of course you are. That's a part of your job." I stared right back at him.

Campbell shook his head. "Tell me everything."

"I just told Saracen what happened."

"I want to hear it. What time did you find the body?"

"We've been here ten minutes at the most. I met Princess Alice when she was drawing in the garden while I was out with Meatball. She suggested a walk, so we headed into the woods."

"Why the woods? Why this area in particular?"

"No reason. Meatball led the way. He took off, and Princess Alice chased him. I was running to catch up with them when I discovered her passed out."

"This is a large area. Why did you lead Princess Alice here?"

I lifted my chin and glared at him. "I didn't! It was an accident that we stumbled across the body."

Campbell's eyes narrowed. "Not many people come in this area. It's not well-maintained."

"Which is exactly why I use it. Meatball loves to root around and chase squirrels. This is the perfect place for him."

His nostrils flared. "It's no place for a princess."

I lifted a hand. "She's the boss. Besides, we're friends. There was no reason to think it strange that she wanted to come this way."

"Oh! Where's Holly?" Alice gasped as she tried to sit up.

Saracen hovered a hand in front of her, ready to grab her if she fainted again.

"I'm right here." I glanced at Campbell before hurrying to her side. "Everything's okay. Your security team is here now."

Her bottom lip trembled and tears fell from her eyes. "Please don't tell me that was Rupert in the ground. When I saw the hand, I panicked. It's not my brother, is it?"

I grabbed her hand and squeezed. "No, I promise you, it's not him. Rupert's safe."

Campbell loomed over me. "How would you know that? Only the killer would know who that is in the ground."

I shook my head. "Not true. The ring on the little finger doesn't belong to Lord Rupert. He never wears silver rings. And look at those nails. They're far too tidy to be Rupert's. He's always biting his nails."

Alice sighed. "You're right! My brother's a terrible nail biter. He has been since we were children. Are you sure it's not him?"

"As sure as I can be without seeing the face. Unless he's had a manicure in the last twenty-four hours, that's not Lord Rupert."

She hugged me. "I'm so relieved. But who's the poor man who's been buried?"

Campbell touched the small comms device on his ear. "Alpha one to Beta three, I need a location check on Lord Rupert."

I resisted the urge to roll my eyes. "I'm telling you, it's not him."

"I believe you," Alice whispered.

Campbell remained motionless as he waited for Beta three to respond.

"Maybe we should see who's in the ground," Alice said. "Has anyone checked the person is actually dead?"

"I can confirm that the individual isn't alive," Campbell said. "No pulse."

"Oh! How awful." More tears fell from Alice's eyes. "I can't believe it. In my own home. What do you think happened, Holly?"

I glanced at the hand before looking away. "I have no idea. But if you wanted to hide a body, this isn't a bad place to do it."

"How would you know that?" Campbell asked.

"You've already answered that question for me. Barely anyone comes in here. This is one of the wildlife areas in the grounds. It's left for nature to enjoy, not people. It's out of bounds to the public. I only know about it because I work here."

Campbell grunted softly. "Which means that whoever put the body in the ground most likely has an association with the castle."

Alice's hand flew to her mouth. "Somebody I know did this?"

I shook my head. "We don't know that for certain. Whoever killed this person might have had a lucky break and stumbled on this area. Campbell's making assumptions."

"The right kind of assumptions," he said sharply. "Beta three, any sign of Lord Rupert?"

My stomach tightened as Beta three replied with a negative.

Sweat broke out on my top lip. Where was Rupert? I was certain that wasn't him in the ground, but if he couldn't be located, maybe something bad had happened to him as well. Could there be a killer on the loose in the castle grounds and Rupert had gotten in the way? Could he be another victim we'd yet to discover?

Horrible thoughts flew through my head as we waited for confirmation of Rupert's whereabouts.

Alice swiped at the tears on her cheeks. Meatball hopped on her knees and helped to lick her cheeks clean.

She wrapped him in a tight hug as he draped his stubby legs over her shoulder, offering her some much needed comfort.

"Alpha one, this is Beta three. I have confirmation that Lord Rupert is in the castle."

"And he's safe?" Campbell asked.

"Affirmative."

"Alpha one out." Campbell lowered his arm. "It looks like you were right, Miss Holmes. Fortunately for you, this isn't Lord Rupert."

I gritted my teeth. "I appreciate your belief in me."

"Alpha one, this is Beta three."

"Go ahead," Campbell said.

"I've been informed by Lord Rupert that one of his party is missing."

Campbell glanced at me. "Who is it?"

"Kendal Jakes."

"How long has he been missing?"

There was a moment of silence. "No one's seen him since last night."

"Copy that." Campbell stared at the hand poking out of the ground.

I did likewise. Kendal Jakes wasn't missing anymore. I recalled that when I'd met him in the games room, he'd had silver rings on his fingers. That had to be him.

When I looked back at Campbell, he was glaring at me. I gulped loudly and focused back on Alice.

I didn't like that glare for one single second. Campbell thought I was involved in this murder. I should have kept my mouth shut. My stepmom always said I was too observant for my own good. Now, it had gotten me in real trouble.

Still, I refused to be cowed by Campbell and let him think I was involved in this. Even if I had to solve this murder myself, I was going to prove my innocence.

Chapter 8

"Saracen, escort Princess Alice back to the castle," Campbell said.

Saracen nodded and held a hand out for Princess Alice to take.

She kept a tight grip on my hand as she stood slowly, pulling herself up using Saracen's not insubstantial muscles. She swayed from side to side as we both held onto her.

"Promise me you'll stay with me," she said. "I can't bear to be alone right now. I don't feel safe."

"You're perfectly safe, Princess," Campbell said. "I've alerted the alpha and beta security teams. We've doubled the patrols around the castle."

"What about in these trees?" she whispered. "What if the killer is watching us right now?"

"You have nothing to worry about," Campbell said. "I've done a survey of the perimeter. There's nobody nearby."

"What about signs of somebody leaving the area?" I asked. "Any footprints or trails leading out of the woods?"

Campbell stared at me for a long, uncomfortable second. "There are several tracks. I'm certain that two of them will be yours and Princess Alice's footprints."

"Any others?" I asked.

"I have a team on the way. We'll do a complete search."

"Oh, of course. Campbell, you're so good at this sort of thing," Alice said. "Still, it's horribly worrying."

"Which is why you need to get inside the safety of the castle walls," Campbell said. "Saracen won't leave your side."

"Yes, thank you. I appreciate that," Alice said. "And of course, Holly, you must stay with me as well."

Campbell opened his mouth as if to protest but then snapped it shut and nodded. "Whatever you need, Princess."

I didn't miss the sharp glare Campbell gave me. He still thought I was involved. I might have discovered the body and had almost smacked him around the head with a large stick, not that he'd noticed my attack attempt, but it made no sense that I'd lead Alice straight to a body I'd buried in the woods.

My stomach tightened. Unless he thought I'd lured her here to kill her too.

I shook my head as I slowly walked beside Alice, Saracen helping to keep her on her feet.

After the fifth time Alice almost fell, I glanced over her head at Saracen. "Perhaps you should carry the princess back to the castle."

"Oh, I don't want to be a burden," she said. "I really am feeling so lightheaded though. I'm not sure I can make it another step."

Saracen's eyes widened for a second before he nodded. "I can carry you, Princess. If you'll permit me to."

"You have my permission," she said.

Without a word, Saracen scooped an arm under Princess Alice's knees and lifted her as if she weighed nothing more than a bag of sugar.

"Ooooh! You have strong arms." Alice swung her legs. "Holly, you must get Campbell to carry you."

I glanced over my shoulder to where Campbell was following a few paces behind. "Oh, that's not necessary. I feel fine." Even if I was feeling faint, there'd be no way I'd fall into Campbell's arms. He probably wouldn't catch me.

"Are you quite sure?" Alice said. "It's fun being carried by such a big, strong man."

I looked back at Campbell again. For a second, I detected the flicker of a smile crossing his face, but then the usual blank veneer snapped back into place.

"Campbell has better things to do than carry me. After all, he needs to figure out who killed Kendal," I said.

"I can always order him to carry you," Alice said. "That's what the security team is here for. To protect me and my friends at all costs."

I raised a hand. "Nope. Thanks for the offer though. Maybe another time."

That comment earned me a snort from Campbell as he joined us. "Let's get back to the castle. My team is on its way."

We walked the rest of the way in silence. My head was spinning with what I'd just seen. Kendal Jakes had been murdered. And whoever had done it had taken the time to bury him in the castle grounds.

When I'd met Kendal, he hadn't made me think warm and friendly thoughts about him, but he must have done something truly shocking to end up murdered and slung in a shallow grave.

The whole time we walked, Campbell scouted the area as the evening gloom grew around us.

The tension drifting off him only made me sweat more. I was a bundle of nerves and jumped every time the wind blew.

I didn't know much about Campbell's background, but he'd served in the military. He must be used to seeing dead bodies and dealing with situations like this, but I wasn't. I wanted to forget all about it, but my mind wouldn't let it go.

And if Campbell thought I had anything to do with this, I needed to make sure the killer was caught as quickly as possible.

"Take me through to the lady's parlor," Alice said. "I need a sit down and some strong tea."

Saracen nodded and led the way as we entered through a side door in the castle. We strode along several corridors before he pushed open the door and walked into a pastel blue parlor. The room was set up with a number of comfortable armchairs and sofas. There was a round table, several bookcases, and a large ornate fireplace. It was Princess Alice's favorite room; she could often be found in here.

Saracen placed her carefully down and helped her into a seat.

She collapsed with an audible oomph before patting the cushions behind her.

"I'll go get some tea," I said.

"No! Please don't leave me," Alice said.

"Campbell and Saracen are here," I said. "You're perfectly safe. Much safer with two trained killers than you are with little old me and Meatball."

"Even so, I don't want to be on my own." She held a hand out and her eyes filled with tears.

Of course I wasn't going to abandon my friend in her time of need. I hurried to her side, grabbed her hand, and settled in the seat next to her.

Meatball jumped up on the sofa and snuggled in tight between us.

"Saracen, be an angel and go to the kitchen. Arrange for us to have some tea," Alice said. "And you must get some for yourselves too. And some sweet tarts. After a shock like this, everyone needs sugar. Get enough for all of us. You must join me."

"That's very kind of you, Princess," Campbell said. "We're trained to deal with this kind of situation. We won't take tea and cake with you. We have a killer to locate."

She smoothed a hand over her muddy dress. "Oh, well, if you're certain. A brandy, then?"

He shook his head. "Thank you. We're fine as we are. We have to keep a clear head. Saracen, make sure Princess Alice gets what she needs."

Saracen simply nodded and left the room, returning a moment later.

It was only a couple of minutes before Sally Elliott bustled in with a tray of china cups and a plate of delicate fancy tarts. I noticed they weren't ones I'd made. They must be Chef Heston's creations.

Sally poured the tea, shooting me a curious glance as Princess Alice passed around the cakes, insisting both Campbell and Saracen have one.

I took several deep breaths. I couldn't fight the worry building inside me. As much as I tried to keep calm, I was freaking out. I was a new face in the castle. I'd been here less than three months. People were still getting to know me, and although I made friends easily, what if the finger of suspicion remained pointed at me?

Kendal had been a bit handsy with me when we'd met. I'd done my best to brush him off and be polite about doing it, but if Campbell found out about that, it would look suspicious. Maybe he'd think I'd taken offense at Kendal's behavior and done something about it.

I bit my lip and concentrated on my tea, trying to keep my hand steady as I took a sip.

The door burst open, and I jumped. Rupert raced into the room, his frantic gaze darting around. He ran to his sister and engulfed her in a huge hug.

"I just heard what happened. You really found Kendal in the woods?"

Alice patted his back. "I did! It was terrible. Meatball led us straight to him. He was trying to dig your friend up. I think he was trying to save him."

I wasn't so sure about that. Meatball had a thing for pungent smells, and there wasn't much more pungent than a body slowly rotting in the ground.

Rupert pulled back and turned to me. He opened his arms as if to hug me too but then froze. His cheeks flushed bright pink, and he lowered his arms.

"Holly! This must be such a shock for you as well." He awkwardly patted my head several times. "How are you?"

"Okay. Much like your sister, still a bit stunned by what we discovered."

He stopped patting my head and stood. "You must be. What on earth happened? What did you see in the woods?"

Campbell cleared his throat. "Sir, I will be questioning all the witnesses individually. Most likely a murder has been committed."

"When are the police getting here?" I asked. "I was about to call them after we discovered the body, but then I heard you in the woods."

"And decided to attack me with a branch, instead of getting help?" Campbell asked.

"I didn't know it was you. I thought the killer had come back. I was protecting Princess Alice."

"Perhaps I should recruit you to my security team, since you seem so intent on keeping the household safe," Campbell said.

I lifted my chin and met his gaze directly, not missing his sarcasm. "I might not be trained like your team, but I wasn't going to let some evil ne'er-do-well harm either of us."

"That was so brave of you, Holly," Alice said. "I was such a ninny and fainted. I'd have been completely vulnerable if you hadn't been there."

"Yes! You're a hero, Holly," Rupert said. "Protecting my sister like that. You should get a medal."

I glanced at Campbell and couldn't help but feel a little smug. "A medal won't be necessary. I'm so sorry about what happened to your friend."

"As am I," Rupert said with a shake of his head. "We all thought it was strange when he didn't show for the shooting this morning. He drank a lot last night. I knocked on his door several times but got no reply. I figured he was sleeping it off."

Campbell cleared his throat again. "We'll take things from here, sir."

I tilted my head. "What do you mean? Why aren't the police coming to interview us?"

"Because we're taking the lead," Campbell said. "We have full jurisdiction here."

That didn't sound right to me. "I don't get it. A crime's been committed. Surely the police have to be involved."

"Oh, don't worry, Holly," Alice said. "They will be. Campbell knows what he's doing."

"Thank you," he said. "And yes, I have informed the police as to what's occurred, but my private security team is taking the lead on this."

"Campbell's incredible at this sort of thing." Alice smiled and fluttered her lashes at him. "He's a highly trained former agent. Campbell's been all over the world on secret missions for the government. Of course, he'll tell you he hasn't, but I've seen his file. Mommy only employs the best agents to protect us. I'm sure if you gave him a plastic spoon, he could kill you with it in a dozen ways. Isn't that right, Campbell?"

He let out a quiet sigh. "I am trained in all forms of defense and attack. I'm sure I could figure out how to do something with a plastic spoon."

I regarded him with interest. "And you're really taking the lead on this investigation?"

"I'll be working alongside the local police," he said. "We have an agreement in place. They're kept informed of all pertinent information. They have no problems with this."

They might not, but I did. Campbell sounded like the kind of guy who could make you disappear if you got on his wrong side. Right now, that was the exact side I was on, and I didn't like it.

I gobbled down a lemon tart, barely tasting the tangy perfection as I tried to slow my racing heart. Campbell might be looking at me as the prime suspect in this investigation. I had to convince him that I was innocent.

"I'll start by questioning Holly," Campbell said.

I grimaced. It was like my worst nightmare coming true.

"You'll be fine." Alice patted my hand. "Just tell him everything you saw. We'll catch whoever did this."

I stood, and Meatball made to come with me. "No, stay and comfort Princess Alice."

Meatball whined and nudged me with his nose. "Woof."

"Be a good boy. She needs comforting."

"Woof woof." Reluctantly he remained with Alice.

I tried to appear calm as I followed Campbell out of the parlor and into an empty room along the corridor. It was a family study with a large desk, bookshelves, and a chaise lounge in one corner.

Campbell gestured to a seat, and I sat in it. He remained standing. That only made me nervous.

I shifted in my seat. "Shouldn't we be recording this or something?"

"We are."

I looked around but saw no signs of a recording device. He probably had the entire castle bugged. "So, what do you want to know?"

"Tell me about you."

I hadn't expected that. That felt more like a first date question than the start of an interrogation. "You mean, where I grew up, that kind of thing?"

"I want to get to know the real Holly Holmes."

Who did he think he'd been meeting until today, the fake version of me? I rested my hands on my lap. "I grew up in the seaside town of Broadstairs in Kent. I went to the local school, studied a fun history degree in Hampshire, and then on to catering college. I opened a café in the village when I moved here."

"Why here?"

My brow wrinkled. "Audley St. Mary? It's one of the most beautiful places in the country. It's a tourist hotspot thanks to Audley Castle. I went to a catering college in Cambridgeshire, so it's a location I know well."

"Had you visited the castle before you decided to set up in the village?"

"Several times. It's such a big place that it's easy to come back and find something new. And the gardens are always changing with the seasons, so there's always something new to look at."

"Were your ambitions always to get a position in the castle?"

"No! I mean, I love my job here, but I also loved my café. And it was working until that hideous chain café came to the village and stole my business. I had no choice but to close and look for something else."

Campbell blinked slowly. "What about your friends and family around here?"

"No family around here. Not much family to speak of at all, actually. I have friends. I mean, the people I work with in the kitchen are nice, and I'm fond of Princess Alice."

"Tell me about your friendship with the princess," he said. "She seems to rely on you. Is that something you've engineered since you started working here?"

"Engineered! You make it sound as if I deliberately set out to befriend her. It didn't happen like that. Princess Alice is a sweet person. She's easy to like."

"Employees shouldn't go around becoming overly familiar with members of the household."

Why was he pulling apart my background and my friendships? He couldn't seriously think I'd wangled my way into the castle just to make friends with the family?

I took a steadying breath. "I like Princess Alice. She's a kind person. She's the one who pursued the friendship. I'm very happy to be her friend."

"And Lord Rupert?"

My eyes narrowed. "What about him?"

"You're also friends with him?"

"I believe so. Again, he's a lovely man." I licked my dry lips. "You know all of this. I know you like to keep a low profile, but I see you around."

"Is that because you're watching the security teams' movements?"

I tipped my head back and sighed. "Absolutely not, but I see you patrolling. You're always around the castle or outside making sure everything's secure."

"You shouldn't see that. My teams are designed to be discreet."

"And you are," I said. "I'm sure I miss most of what you do. But now and again, I notice you. That's not a crime."

"It could be associated with a crime if you became familiar with our movements so you could achieve something untoward."

"Like what?"

"Murder Kendal Jakes."

"For goodness sake! I didn't do it."

"Tell me about your relationship with Kendal."

I wiped my sweaty palms on my pants. "There's nothing to tell."

"You do know who he is?"

"A friend of Lord Rupert's," I said. "I met him for the first time when he arrived at the castle and I served desserts."

"And how did that meeting go?"

"It was a short meeting."

"Did you speak to Kendal?"

This was the tricky bit. Did I reveal everything or keep quiet about the fact Kendal had made inappropriate advances toward me? "I did."

"And what did you talk about?"

"My desserts."

"Kendal Jakes is the son of Earl Stephen Jakes. He's a notable member of the House of Lords. A powerful man."

"I had no idea. Do you think that's relevant to his murder?"

Campbell was silent for a long moment. "What else did you talk about?"

"Nothing! Although …" If I concealed things, it would only add to Campbell's belief I was guilty. But if I told the truth, it gave me a motive for killing Kendal. Not a strong one, but it might be all Campbell needed to keep hounding me.

"Go on."

"Kendal had been drinking when we met. He said a few… inappropriate things. Lord Rupert had to warn him off. It was nothing serious."

"He said inappropriate things to you?" Campbell's chest expanded as he took a deep breath. "He propositioned you?"

"Barely! Like I said, he was drinking and showing off to his friends. It was nothing I couldn't handle."

"Maybe you handled him when you saw him again," Campbell said. "Did Kendal pursue you and things got out of hand?"

"No! That was the only time I saw Kendal. I figured I'd never see him again."

"Where were you last night?" he asked.

"In my staff apartment," I said.

"Alone?"

"No, I was with Meatball."

"That's not an acceptable alibi."

"It's the only one I've got. It's my usual routine. I can assure you, I didn't kill Kendal." Despite protesting my innocence, I felt guilty. Maybe it was the way Campbell was interrogating me. He was trying to strip apart my life and find a fault, find a reason for me to turn into a killer. But he wasn't going to beat me.

"I'll check where you were," he said. "But for now, you're free to go."

"You're really going to lead on this investigation?" I asked.

He stared at me without blinking. "Correct. It won't be the first time I've had a criminal matter to investigate. As Princess Alice so kindly revealed, I do have experience in this area."

"Were you in the military police?"

He didn't reply.

"Maybe you really were in MI5. Does that give you experience with investigating murders?"

There wasn't a flicker of response. It was like he'd turned to stone.

I sighed as I stood. "Don't you want to know about the body?"

"You've already told me everything when we were in the woods. My team is investigating the scene now. If I have any further questions, I'll be sure to come find you. After all, I know where you live."

That was hardly reassuring.

As I reached the door, Campbell caught hold of my arm. "Don't do anything foolish, Miss Holmes. This is a murder investigation. Stay out of the way."

"So long as you don't charge me with anything, I'm happy to do just that." I hurried out the room, Campbell right on my heels, and returned to find Alice and Rupert sitting together, Saracen guarding them.

"If I may have a word with you now, Lord Rupert," Campbell said.

"Oh! Of course." He stood and ran a hand through his hair. "We need to find out who did this to Kendal. I won't be long." He patted his sister's shoulder before striding out with Campbell.

I sat next to Alice, my insides shaking like they were made out of jelly.

"Don't mind Campbell and his questions." She grabbed my hand. "Are you okay? You're white like a ghost."

"Of course." I took a breath and tried to relax. "Campbell's just being thorough. We found the body, after all."

"I trust Campbell, but he does keep looking at you strangely. I'd hate to think he considers you a suspect."

I forced a smile. "Campbell doesn't scare me."

"You're so brave, Holly. Here, have another lemon tart." Alice passed me the almost empty plate.

I took one and nodded a thanks. I was glad she believed my blatant lie. I was terrified of Campbell. Just as I was terrified he might be planning to put me behind bars for a very long time.

Chapter 9

I paced the length of the lady's parlor for what felt like the hundredth time. Campbell had been questioning Princess Alice for more than fifteen minutes. Surely she couldn't know that much about Kendal.

Maybe he was using the same tactic he'd done on me, trying to make everyone sweat in the hope they'd let something slip.

He couldn't believe for one second that Alice had anything to do with what happened to Kendal.

Maybe this was simply how Campbell operated. He considered everyone guilty until he'd proven otherwise.

The door opened. Campbell entered first, followed by Alice.

Her cheeks looked flushed, but other than that she seemed fine. She hurried over and grabbed my hand. "Goodness! He was very thorough. I almost felt like I'd done something wrong."

I glanced at Campbell, who stood motionless by the door.

"I'll leave you for a moment, ladies." Campbell pushed the door closed as he stepped outside.

"How did it go?" I led Alice to a seat, and we both sat.

She kept a tight hold of my hand. "He mainly wanted to know all about Kendal."

"Did you know him well?"

"Not particularly. He was always hanging around with my brother when we were younger. I never thought all that much of him to be honest."

"Why is that?"

"He was always showing off about something. He had to have the most expensive watch or the latest designer brand of shoes. Some girls were impressed by that, but not me. I always thought he was a bit … crass. And I know that makes me sound like a terrible snob. Maybe I am a bit, but it seemed Kendal always had something to prove."

"How was his friendship with Lord Rupert?"

"Rupert always laughed things off, but Kendal was mean to him, and not in a jokey way. He used to pick on him. My brother was a bit of a weed when he was a teenager. He was all gangly arms and legs and no muscle. Ha! I guess some things never change. Kendal used to tease him and call him a beanpole. Rupert pretended it didn't bother him, but I could tell it did."

I frowned. That sounded like bullying. "If they weren't really friends, why did Lord Rupert even invite him to this weekend?"

Alice sighed. "Holly, you're so lucky. You never had to endure all the nonsense we did when growing up."

"You mean all the luxurious dinners, top-rate education, a finishing school in Vienna, and five-star holidays on private sandy beaches. How did you cope?"

She pinched my arm. "Meany! I meant, all the out-of-date traditional rules about etiquette, who you needed to be friends with, and what school you had to go to. The old boys' network is very much alive and kicking. Rupert made friends with Kendal and the others when they were at Eton. Our families are all connected and go back hundreds of years. He couldn't ignore Kendal, even if he wasn't really friendly with him. It's bad manners, you see."

"It sounds like a terrible burden having that much privilege and position." I couldn't help but sound a little cynical. Sure, there were a few conventions they needed to stick to, but Alice and Rupert would never need to worry about money. People fell over themselves to give them things and be seen with them. I didn't begrudge either of them that and would hate to be in the limelight like they were, but their positions gave them things most people only got to dream about.

She lightly slapped the back of my hand. "I know you're still teasing me, Holly Holmes. I also know that I'm a very lucky young lady. Still, this luck can be tiresome. My ladies' finishing school was just the same as Eton. Every year, one of us must host an event for the other ladies who graduated from our class. It's so boring. All they want to talk about is their husbands or the men they want to marry. It won't be long before it's baby names and christenings. I'm sticking with dogs." She stroked Meatball, who was fast asleep on the sofa.

"You're not interested in finding a husband and making lots of pretty babies?"

"One day. But when I marry, it will be for love. I'm just like the heroine in that Jane Austen book. What's her name?"

"Emma? She was always interfering and matchmaking."

"Hush now! I'm nothing like Emma. Miss Elizabeth Bennett. I'm marrying for love and not money."

"In your position, you can marry whoever you like," I said.

"The chance would be a fine thing." She plucked at the sleeve of her dress. "Mommy is still suggesting men she considers suitable matches for me, despite my poor track record on that front. They've either got weak chins, crossed eyes, or less sense than I have. It puts me right off the idea of getting married. Perhaps I'll remain a spinster forever. And if I do, you're coming with me."

"You want me to be a spinster alongside you?"

She laughed heartily. "Absolutely! You can be my baking spinster, and I can get fat and wrinkled while I eat all your delicious desserts."

I tipped my head from side to side. That wasn't a terrible idea. Alice would be a joy to work for. "I tell you what, if we both hit fifty and neither of us is married, it's a deal."

"I won't let you back out on that," she said. "We must shake on it to seal the deal."

I stuck my hand out and grinned. "Happy to do so."

She grabbed my hand and squeezed. "And, if you break your word, I have the authority to order your head to be chopped off. There's still a working guillotine in the Tower of London, I believe."

I swiftly withdrew my hand. Sometimes, Alice had a dark side to her humor. It often involved taking off people's heads. Did she really have the power to send me to the Tower of London? I shook my head, which was firmly attached to my neck, just where I liked it.

"It won't come to that," I said lightly. "Some lucky guy will sweep you off your feet before you know it."

"And yours. You're such a catch with all your skills in the kitchen."

"I hope some man marries me for more than my ability to cook!"

"And I hope some man decides to marry me and overlook the fact I can't sew, draw, or play the piano."

We both laughed. Our backgrounds were so different, but somehow we just clicked.

"Getting back to what happened to Kendal," I said. "The Duchess mentioned that Rupert had a tough time when he was at school. Was it only Kendal who bullied him?"

"I never got to see much of what happened. It's an all boys' school and they don't let girls inside. I attended some presentations they held for family members, but that was about it."

"Is it possible he was the ring leader of a bigger group?" It made me sick to think of Rupert being picked on.

"It's possible. Kendal wasn't a nice man." Alice ruffled Meatball's fur. "He probably deserved what happened to him."

"Alice! No one deserves to die and be buried in a shallow grave."

"You might change your mind when you learn a bit more about Kendal Jakes." She lifted her chin. "But perhaps you're right. He made a big mistake this time. He got on the wrong side of someone mean."

"I'm sure he's regretting it now."

The door to the lady's parlor opened, and Campbell returned. "You may both leave."

Alice shot me a sharp look. "How kind of you, Campbell, to tell me how I may move around my own home."

He inclined his head. "Your safety and well-being is always a priority, Princess."

She sniffed and stood before smoothing her hands over her dress. "Very well. I'm exhausted. I'll see you in the morning, Holly." She sashayed out of the room.

I expected Campbell to turn and follow her, but he remained by the open door, his gaze on me.

I petted Meatball's head as he woke, and pretended not to notice Campbell, uncomfortable under his scrutiny.

I couldn't put it off any longer. I stood and nodded at Campbell. "I'll turn in for the night too."

He caught hold of my arm as I reached the door. "You need to be careful."

I stared up at him. He was way too tall. He must be at least six foot five. "About what?"

"Don't get involved with this. I understand that you found the body and it must have been a shock, but stay out of it. You're still considered a suspect."

"You're wasting your time looking at me. I didn't kill Kendal."

"Maybe that's so, and by the morning I'll have checked your alibi and discounted you from the list, providing you're innocent."

"How long a list do you have?" I asked. "You must be interviewing Kendal's friends. Does anyone there have a reason to want him dead?"

"That's none of your business. Stop poking around and asking questions."

"I haven't been asking any questions."

He arched an eyebrow. "Really? You weren't just talking to Princess Alice about what she knew about Kendal?"

I glanced around the room. He really must have this place bugged. "You can't blame me for wanting to get to the bottom of this."

"I don't blame you; I'm just telling you to stay out of it. I'll handle things from here. You keep your head down and your nose clean, or you'll look guilty."

I gritted my teeth and resisted telling him again that I had nothing to do with this. "Come on, Meatball, let's go to bed. That's if it's allowed."

Campbell released his firm grip on my arm and stepped back. "Of course. This is for your own safety. Assuming you're innocent, there's a killer on the loose, and it's quite likely they're still around. You don't want them to learn that you're asking questions about what happened to Kendal. If they do, you may be the next victim."

I swallowed as I hurried away with Meatball. Of course I didn't want that. But I also didn't want to wait under a cloud of suspicion while Campbell did his job.

First thing in the morning, I'd get this sorted out once and for all.

I was already settled at the kitchen table and enjoying a fresh out of the oven blueberry muffin topped with crystalized brown sugar when Betsy Malone strode through the door.

Betsy had worked in the castle for over twenty years. She was the head housekeeper and oversaw a team of forty cleaners. They ensured the castle was in tiptop condition, not only for the tourists but also for the residents.

Her broad face brightened when she saw me. "Have you heard the news?"

"About what was found in the woods?" I popped a piece of muffin in my mouth.

"One of Lord Rupert's friends, so everyone's saying." She placed her metal carrier of neatly lined up cleaning supplies on the floor, washed her hands, and then helped herself to a muffin.

"Actually, I found the body."

Her dark eyes widened. "Oh! You poor thing. What a terrible shock. What was it like? What did you see? Was the body horribly maimed? Was there a lot of blood?"

I couldn't help but grin. Betsy loved nothing more than a good gossip. And she got all the best information. Her team of cleaners were trained to be discreet and silent as they went about their duties. Betsy taught them everything they knew. If I didn't know better, I'd say she was a spy herself. She had a way of popping up when you least expected her.

"I was with Princess Alice and Meatball. We saw Kendal Jakes's hand poking out of the ground. Then the chaos started. Campbell and Saracen turned up, we were all escorted back to the castle, and then the questioning began."

"Well I never! What would they be questioning you about?" She slapped her hands on her wide hips and stared hard at me. "They can't think you're a suspect."

"I reckon Campbell thinks everyone's guilty of doing something they shouldn't." I lowered my voice and glanced over my shoulder. Campbell also had an uncanny knack of turning up when you least wanted him to.

"Did you know Kendal?" Betsy asked.

"Never met him until a couple of days ago. He must have gotten on someone's bad side."

"I should say he did." She tutted and shook her head. "And Lord Rupert, losing one of his friends like that. Such a shame. It breaks your heart. He's a good man."

"He is," I said. "Have you been in to clean Kendal's room today?"

"I tried, but I was sent away. Campbell's got it under guard. I was told it's a potential crime scene."

"Does he think something bad happened to Kendal in his room?"

"Maybe so; I couldn't get a real look. Not that it matters much. I had to clean the room after he arrived. He'd left it in such a mess. I could easily have swept away important evidence. I'm not taking the blame for that. I didn't know he'd be killed."

"What was his room like?"

"The place was a pigsty. For someone who was supposed to be from the upper class, he had absolutely no manners."

"What did you find?"

"Damp towels thrown on the floor, underwear not put away, an open bottle of whiskey, and a half-eaten sandwich. Oh, and there was a shirt thrown on the floor with lipstick on the collar."

"Kendal had a woman with him?"

"He must have, unless he liked to wear women's makeup in private." She slapped a hand on her thigh. "Imagine that! Of course, I've seen much worse. This posh lot get up to all sorts behind closed doors. I once catered for a party of swingers."

"Swingers?"

"Yes! It was before my time working here. They all put their keys in a glass bowl and selected a partner for the night. I was so shocked I didn't know where to look. Still, the pay was good and all in cash, so I chose to look the other way. Kendal wearing lipstick wouldn't shock me. Not much does these days. Not when you've been around as long as I have."

I didn't recall seeing lipstick on Kendal's collar when I'd met him. "What color was the shirt?"

"Pale blue. It was crumpled and several of the buttons were missing as if he'd taken it off in a hurry. Oh! Maybe it was a romantic tryst. He was getting amorous with this woman and things got out of hand."

I tapped my fingers on the kitchen table. His friends had mentioned that he was involved with a married woman, and someone else. Izzie, I think they'd said when Kendal was being teased about his complicated love life.

Betsy finished her muffin and smacked her lips together. "Delicious."

My thoughts remained on Kendal and this elusive woman. Maybe a jealous girlfriend was behind what had happened to him. He could have snuck this woman in, had some fun with her, and then sent her away.

I was just reaching for a second muffin when Campbell and Chef Heston strode in together.

"Gossiping again, Miss Holmes?" Campbell's gaze went from Betsy to me.

"I never gossip," Betsy said. "It's not nice to talk about people behind their backs."

Chef Heston glowered at me. "Get to work, or I'll put a warning on your record. And you were late getting back from your deliveries yesterday. If any of the customers report that the food was stale, I'll dock your wages. And you'll need to stay late today. I've got a rush job on."

Campbell cleared his throat. "Actually, Holly's been helping me with inquiries regarding a ... family matter. Her working hours will need to be flexible in the short-term so she can commit to providing the family with everything they need."

My mouth dropped open, and Chef Heston spluttered several words.

"I trust that won't be a problem." Campbell turned his full, scary attention to Chef Heston.

"Of course not, if it's to assist the family." He tightened his apron string around his waist and stepped back. "I simply haven't been informed about this."

I opened my mouth to protest, but one glance from Campbell had me keeping quiet. Was he standing up for me? Why would he do that? He'd made it clear that he didn't think much of me.

"In fact, I have a few questions I need to ask you." Campbell grabbed Chef Heston by the shoulder and led him away.

"You need to be careful of that one," Betsy said quietly once the door had closed.

"Chef Heston or Campbell? They both terrify me in their own particular ways."

"I've heard things about Campbell that'll turn your blood to ice. That man is scary. He used to be a secret agent. He got so deep undercover on one mission that he forgot who he really was. The government lost all trace of him for almost a year until he resurfaced. He had to go through intensive rehabilitation before he was deemed fit to return to duty. And I've heard he can speak seven different languages."

"Only seven," I said.

Betsy snorted a laugh. "Watch your back around him. Campbell's like a dog with his favorite bone. When he gets the scent of something and thinks he's right, he won't let it drop."

Campbell returned to the kitchen, minus Chef Heston.

"What did you do with him, hang his body in the deep freeze?" I asked.

"That's too obvious a hiding place," Campbell said. "He won't be a problem anymore. I informed him that I need you available for questioning at a moment's notice."

Betsy pursed her lips and stared at me, warning and worry in her gaze.

"So, my alibi didn't check out?" I asked.

"You don't have much of an alibi." He grabbed a muffin and left.

Betsy tutted again. "Mark my words, no good will come of an association with that man. You steer clear of Campbell." She bustled off with her cleaning materials.

I stared at the plate of muffins and smiled. Maybe he wasn't as scary and impenetrable as he wanted everyone to believe. If Campbell had a sweet tooth, then I had the perfect weapon to break down his defenses.

I washed up, pulled out my favorite dessert recipe book, and laid out the ingredients for the perfect salted caramel buttercream mini layered sponges.

It was time to work on getting Campbell on my side and making sure he knew that I was innocent.

Chapter 10

It was fortunate that I had no deliveries to make that morning, and I spent the whole time baking batches of bread, rolls, and cakes to sell to the tourists at lunchtime.

Whenever I had a break, I finished working on the cakes to give to Campbell. He may have been able to speak multiple languages and kill a person with a plastic spoon, but he'd never beat me when it came to killer desserts. Everyone had a weakness when it came to pudding, and I was great at remembering what made a person drool with desire.

With most of the baking and food preparation done for the lunchtime rush, I had time on my hands.

Chef Heston was out dealing with a delivery, most likely yelling at the poor driver for being late. That gave me an opportunity to pull out my sponges and finish them off with a drizzle of dark melted chocolate and a pinch of sea salt to enhance the caramel tang.

Stepping back, I ran my gaze over them. They were just like tiny delicate works of art. Now, all I needed to do was find Campbell and sweeten him up with them. Prove that I wasn't a bad person.

I placed the cakes in a tin and secured the lid before heading outside. Campbell had made several circuits of the castle during the morning, and I'd seen him sweep past the kitchen windows on more than one occasion. Maybe he was still outside.

After walking around for a good ten minutes, there was no sign of him or his team. Perhaps they were in the woods.

I hesitated at the edge of the lawn. I didn't dare risk going back to the scene of the crime. It could make me look guilty.

Laughter drifted toward me. I turned and spotted Lord Rupert with the gardening team.

I headed toward them, and he waved as he saw me. I hadn't had much of a chance to speak to him last night and wanted to check he was doing okay.

"Hey, everyone." I stopped by the newly planted garden. "This looks amazing." A huge newly turned flower bed was full of fragrant herbs. I wasn't a gardening expert, but I knew my herbs. There was thyme, parsley, sage, and lavender on display.

Several of the gardeners nodded and smiled at me as they tidied up their tools.

"And it's all thanks to me not having touched a thing." Rupert walked over, a smile on his face. "I've only been advising. I managed to kill half a dozen lavender plants when I transplanted them a couple of weeks ago. I put them in the wrong soil and they went into shock. Then I overwatered them, rotting the roots. So, this time, I stood back and made suggestions about where things should go. And we've done a decent job."

"You're the perfect advisor," one of the gardeners said. "We'll make a professional out of you one day."

"It all looks beautiful." My gaze ran over the myriad of purple and lush green.

"It's a memorial garden," Rupert said. "People can come here where it's quiet to remember lost loved ones. They can even donate to have a plaque put on the ground with their loved one's name on it."

"What a nice idea. Are you thinking about having something put here for Kendal?" I asked.

"Oh! Well, I hadn't thought about that. I mean, it's for loved ones. Family members, really. And, I mean, Kendal was a friend, but ..." His words trailed off and he rubbed the back of his neck.

"Would you like a cake?" I gently led Rupert away from the gardeners so they wouldn't overhear us.

"Golly! These look scrumptious. Did you make them for me?" He peered in the tin, delight in his eyes.

"They're an experiment," I said, not wanting to admit they were a failed bribe for Campbell.

"I'm more than willing to be your experimental guinea pig." He selected a cake and took a bite. He closed his eyes and groaned. "Holly Holmes, you never fail to amaze me."

"You need something to cheer you up after what happened to your friend. I bet you're still in shock."

He finished the cake and licked each finger clean. "You never think someone so young will go so suddenly."

"It's not something I can imagine," I said. "Were you close?"

His smile was rueful. "We shared a dormitory when we were teenagers. You get to see a lot when you share a space with another teenage boy."

I didn't want any details about that. "You were all a part of the same gang, though. You liked hanging out with each other?"

Rupert studied the toes of his muddy boots for several seconds before looking up at me. "If I had my way, I'd never see Kendal Jakes again. Well, I guess I never will now, but I didn't want it to end like this. I didn't want him dead."

Worry swirled through me. "You didn't get on when you were at school?"

"I wasn't always this …" He waved a hand up and down his torso. "I mean to say, people change. Everyone grows at different rates, and sometimes, it takes a while to figure out your way in the world. I was never a natural athlete or hugely academic. My old school was competitive. I felt like I wasn't good enough. That brought me to the attention of people who were better than me. Survival of the fittest you might say."

"You think Kendal was better than you because he was good at sports and got an A grade on his papers?" Irritation made my cheeks flush.

"Oh, it wasn't just that. Kendal had this natural charm with people. He had a way to get anyone to like him. Well, almost anyone."

"You saw through him," I said. "If anything, that makes you the better person. You saw the truth about Kendal. From what I've learned about him, he wasn't a good friend to you."

"Oh, well, I've heard it said before that children can be very cruel. And Kendal was particularly cruel." His gaze was full of guilt. "But I still don't want him dead, and I certainly never killed him."

"I can't imagine you'd ever want to harm anyone." I smiled warmly at him.

"Too much of a wet blanket. My father often used to say that about me. Too soft for my own good."

"No! You're nothing of the sort." I touched his arm. "Kindness is a strength. And you have it in bucket loads. Here, have another cake." I thrust the tin at him.

"You spoil me." Rupert took another cake. "That's very sweet of you."

I wasn't doing it because I felt sorry for him. Rupert was a genuinely nice guy. He was handsome, clever, and always looking out for others. I swiftly stowed those thoughts away. There was no point in getting a crush on a member of the family. "Have you heard how the investigation's going?"

"No, nothing new from Campbell. He's keeping the Duke and Duchess informed."

"He didn't tell me much about what actually happened to Kendal. What did he tell you when you spoke to him?" I asked.

"Oh! He was open with me. Kendal was hit on the head by something hard. He was probably drunk when he was attacked. We told him to pace himself, but Kendal always said he could hold his drink. Hopefully, the alcohol numbed his senses, so he didn't know what was going on. That's what I like to think, anyway."

"What time did Kendal die? Does Campbell know?"

"Between about midnight and two in the morning," Rupert said. "The last time any of us saw him it was around eleven thirty."

That definitely excluded me from being a suspect. I was in my room all night with Meatball from nine. I was an early bird and most productive in the morning. If I was ever going to commit a murder, it would be at dawn when I had my wits about me.

"Did Campbell ask where you were at the time of Kendal's murder?"

"Absolutely. I'd expect nothing less of him. He wouldn't be doing his job properly if he didn't ask where we all were. I'm assuming he asked you as well."

"He did. My alibi's solid. Well, solid in the fact I was home alone."

He chuckled. "Holly, I can't imagine a less likely killer. I was with the other guys. Although there was half an hour when two of them went missing. Campbell was interested in that."

"Why did you split up?"

"Chris and Simon went to the kitchen because they got hungry. I didn't think it was odd. I still don't. No one in the party would want to kill Kendal. He could be jolly annoying, but that was always how he was. We got used to it over the years."

"The night I met Kendal and your friends, you were joking about Kendal being a ladies' man."

"Oh dear. I thought he'd overstepped the mark with you. I suggested he come and apologize, but he was having none of it."

I shook my head. "I'm not bothered about that, but was he seeing anyone special? Maybe someone he snuck into the castle because he couldn't bear to be away from her for a night."

"Kendal with a serious girlfriend?" Rupert tipped back his head and roared with laughter. "That would never happen. Kendal enjoyed the ladies, but he never stuck with the same one for more than a few months. He said why bother settling for just one woman when there were so many out there to enjoy."

"That's an interesting way to think about women." I arched a brow.

Rupert's cheeks flushed. "Of course, I don't think that. I'm waiting for a special lady to come into my life."

I smiled. "I'm sure you are. I don't think that you're a womanizer."

"I'd never dream of doing such a thing," he spluttered out. "The right girl's waiting for me, I know it. I'm just not certain she knows that she's the right one for me."

I looked away as my cheeks grew warm. Rupert was such a sweet guy, and if I'd met him in any other circumstances, I'd have been tempted to pursue something with him. But there was a line you should never cross.

"Getting back to Kendal's relationships, he didn't talk about bringing someone along to your get-together?"

"He said nothing to me. Although he has been seeing someone's wife. And of course, he's been in an on-off relationship with Izzie Northcott for a long time."

"What's the current situation with their relationship?"

"As far as I know, he got rid of her some time ago."

"What did Izzie think about that?"

"I imagine she wasn't happy, but Kendal was good at manipulating her to get what he wanted."

Did Campbell know about Izzie and her relationship with Kendal? How could I tell him there might be a jealous ex-girlfriend on the scene without revealing that I was still poking around and asking questions?

"We're stopping now, if that's okay," one of the gardeners called out.

Rupert raised a hand and nodded at her. "Of course." He walked back toward the gardeners, and I walked alongside him.

"I know this is a terrible business, but Campbell will sort things out," Rupert said. "Try not to worry. This is a one-off. We can't have the castle getting a reputation for being a murder hot spot."

"Absolutely not," I said. "I don't want to start baking cakes for the castle ghosts because the visitors stop turning up." I'd meant it as a joke, but the horror on Rupert's face suggested I'd put my foot in it.

"You really believe the castle is haunted?" he asked.

I chuckled, which died when he didn't join in. "So the guidebooks say. Isn't it?"

Rupert glanced up at the vast stone building. "I ... well, I guess stranger things have happened. And I'm always losing things. When I was younger, I always blamed the ghosts when my toys went missing."

I nodded and leaned closer. "It's the cold spots that get me."

"Oh! You feel them too?"

A clattering sound had me turning. I walked over when I saw a heap of dropped tools. "Let me help with those." I placed the cake tin on the ground.

Meredith and Jacob were hurrying around, picking up the tools.

Meredith pushed her hat back and smiled. "Thanks. I thought I'd be able to get this lot inside in one go. More haste less speed, that's what my mom always used to tell me."

I shifted aside several spades and a hoe that was already in the trunk to make room for everything else. "It looks like you've been busy today."

"I love working on the beds," Meredith said. "You can't beat a bit of exercise in the great outdoors."

"Give it a few months, and that planting will look beautiful," Jacob said as he piled in more tools.

"It already does. Here, you might as well have the rest of these." I handed over the tin of cakes. "I expect the rest of the gardeners have worked up quite an appetite."

"They look great," Jacob said.

"Oooh! Thanks. They'll love these." Meredith hurried away to join the rest of the group and hand over the cakes.

"Holly Holmes!" Chef Heston leaned out the kitchen door, his face red. "Get back to work. You've got deliveries to make this afternoon."

"Oh dear." Rupert hurried over to me. "I hope I haven't got you into trouble by keeping you chatting."

"Don't worry, Chef Heston just enjoys yelling at me. I'll see you later." I dashed back to the kitchen.

I glanced at Rupert as he stood watching the gardeners pack the rest of their equipment away. Dealing with a bully was a good motive for murder. But I couldn't believe Rupert was involved in what had happened, and he had his friends as alibis, although they all sounded like they'd been pretty drunk that night.

I shook my head. Rupert was a kind, sweet guy, not a killer.

I needed to look elsewhere to find out what happened to Kendal Jakes. And my elsewhere had to involve the scorned ex-girlfriend.

Chapter 11

"These hazelnut and dark chocolate truffle tarts look delicious," Mavis Bickerly said as I handed over my final delivery for the day.

"I'm also experimenting with a new cupcake flavor," I said.

Mavis's large dark eyes widened as she peered into the box. "What surprise have you brought me?" She lived alone and ran a book group from her cottage on Cedar Lane. Every month, she placed a generous cake order for her group to enjoy.

"I know you love cupcakes, so I added a few free samples. They're caramel cream and maple roasted pecan. Feedback's welcome. Let me know what you and your book club think of them. I want to get them just right."

"Everything you touch in that kitchen turns out right," Mavis said with a warm smile. She looked over my shoulder. "Still no van?"

"Chef Heston likes me out on the bike. And I don't really mind. It helps burn off all the calories I eat taste testing my cakes."

Mavis chuckled. "Lucky you. I only have to look at this box of cakes and I feel like I've gained five pounds."

"They're worth it." I waved goodbye and headed back to my recently repaired delivery bike which I'd propped against the cottage wall.

Meatball sat waiting patiently in the basket. He wagged his tail when he saw me.

"That's it. Last delivery of the day. How about we head back to the castle and get you some dinner?"

"Woof woof." Meatball bounced in the basket and his tail wagged faster.

A woman I didn't recognize strode toward me, her phone against her ear. Her high nude heels clipped against the ground as she pushed a strand of perfectly blow-dried blonde hair off her heart-shaped face. "And, apparently, the body was discovered in the woods."

I froze and stared at her. She had to be talking about Kendal.

"I'm telling you the truth! My sources are accurate." She glanced at me, and her eyes narrowed. "Hold on just a moment." She didn't say another word until she'd passed me.

I wheeled the bike around and followed her at a discreet distance, making sure I could still hear what she had to say.

"I always knew something like this would happen," the woman said. "He couldn't keep his pants zipped. Someone's angry husband was going to get to him in the end."

This woman clearly had a connection to Kendal. She didn't live in the village, though. I'd never seen her before. Was this one of Kendal's mystery women? Maybe even the woman he'd had inside the castle who'd left the lipstick on his collar. I had to find out.

"I'll have to get somebody else to take me to the Summer Ball." She giggled. "I'm not being cold, I'm being practical. We had it all arranged. I'd even picked out the tuxedo I wanted him to wear. I'll have to start from scratch, and all the best men have already been taken. I'd rather pretend I was sick than go with someone else's ugly cast off."

Whoever this woman was, she didn't seem bothered about Kendal being dead. She was more focused on her social life being inconvenienced.

The woman turned abruptly and stepped out into the road. She stared straight at me and scowled. "I'll call you back." She lowered her phone. "What do you think you're doing?"

I stopped the bike, my cheeks heating. "Nothing! I mean, just riding my bike back to work."

"No you're not." She jabbed a finger at me. "And don't even think about asking for a selfie with me."

"Um, I wasn't going to. I don't know who you are."

She snorted a laugh. "Sure you don't. Didn't anyone ever tell you it's rude to listen into a private conversation?"

"Well, you weren't exactly being private. You were talking very loudly in the middle of a public place."

The woman scowled at me. "Even so, mind your own business. And stay out of mine."

"I didn't mean to overhear, but you mentioned a body in the woods."

Her pink glossed lips pressed together. "Hoping to sell a story to the papers about me being here at the same time as Kendal? That's old news. You won't get a penny for revealing my location. Everyone knows we were an item. Do an image search. We're everywhere."

I had no idea what she was talking about. "I wouldn't know where to start with selling a story to anyone. And if I did that, I'd probably lose my job."

"You're employed?" She looked down her button nose at me. "I thought you were homeless."

"What? No! Why do you think that?" I was in my black pants and jacket I used for cycling in. I might look a bit windswept and pink from cycling around for the last few hours, but homeless!

She shrugged. "It's that greasy hair and flea-bitten dog drooling in your basket that gives you away."

"Meatball isn't flea-bitten. He's very clean. He gets a bath once a week. And I'm not greasy, I'm just a little … sweaty from all the bike riding."

She shooed me away with a manicured hand, although one of the false nails was missing. So, she wasn't Little Miss Perfect after all. "Well, go on. Get on with your deliveries."

I shook my head, refusing to allow her rudeness to deter me. "Did you know Kendal?"

"You're telling me that you knew Kendal Jakes? He wouldn't associate with somebody like you."

I glared at her. "He might. What do you mean by that?"

Meatball growled and gave a single bark.

Her haughty gaze ran over both of us, but there was a flicker of doubt in her blue eyes. "Did you really know Kendal?"

"We've met."

She stepped toward me. "How? Don't tell me you dated. He wouldn't be interested in a sweaty mess like you."

I shrugged the insult off. Riding the bicycle and tugging a cart load of cakes around the village would always work up a sweat. It didn't bother me. I was fit and got to eat cake every day without piling on the pounds.

"I didn't know him in that way. How about you? How did you know Kendal?"

"What makes you think I did?"

"I overheard you say that he was planning to take you to a ball."

"You were listening in!"

It was my turn to shrug. "You were talking loudly."

She scowled at me. "Why the interest in him, anyway?"

"I work at Audley Castle. I—"

"Oh! I understand now. You must be one of the servants."

I sighed. "We're not called servants. This is the twenty-first century. But I do work in the kitchens. I'm—"

The woman stepped closer. "The kitchens! Did you serve Kendal his food? How did he seem?"

"Yes, I served him. He seemed ... drunk."

"Typical. Tell me everything."

Maybe if I shared a little information, this mystery woman might be more forthcoming. "I met him once, the evening before he died."

Her eyes narrowed. "Was he with anyone?"

"Yes. Lord Rupert and his other friends from school."

She waved her hand in the air. "I don't mean the boys. Did he have a woman with him?"

"I didn't see anyone," I said. "Were you two dating?"

"We were close. I had thought we might marry once he'd had his fun."

My eyes widened. "Did you visit Kendal at the castle?"

A smile crossed her face before it vanished. "What a ridiculous idea. How would I be able to get past the castle security?" Her grin returned, suggesting she'd done just that.

"You must be sad about what happened to him. How did you find out?"

Her gaze ran over me. "I am sad. Kendal Jakes would have been a wealthy man when his father finally died."

Wow! This woman was all heart. "You haven't told me your name."

"Nor shall I." Her phone rang, and she checked the caller ID before turning away and answering it. "Jasmine! I was about to call you. I've got some incredible gossip. You're not going to believe this."

"Woof." Meatball growled quietly.

"I couldn't agree more." I petted him on the head and waited, my gaze not leaving the woman as she strolled along the street. She was still chatting on her phone when she turned into the Audley Hotel and disappeared.

I wheeled my bike to the hotel and peeked through the window. There was no sign of her.

"You stay here," I said to Meatball. "Guard the bicycle. If anyone tries to take it, you bark loudly."

"Woof woof."

Not that I worried about my bike being stolen in Audley St. Mary. It was generally a safe village. The most reported crimes involved dropped litter and the occasional owner who didn't pick up after their dog.

I walked into the reception lobby of the hotel and smiled when I saw John Steadman behind the desk. The wall behind him was covered in postcards from places all over the world. John sent them to the hotel whenever he went away.

He'd worked here for three years. It was only supposed to be a summer job before he went traveling full time. What turned into one summer quickly expanded, and he was a permanent fixture at the hotel, spending his three weeks off cramming in as much traveling as possible.

"Holly! What brings you here? Need a room for someone visiting?" A warm smile lit John's clean-shaven face as his brown eyes crinkled at the corners.

"No, actually I'm interested in someone who might be a guest here."

"You want me to reveal secrets about our residents." He waggled his eyebrows. "I'm pretty sure that will break all sorts of confidentiality agreements."

I laughed. "You make it sound like you're working for the Secret Service."

"Sometimes, the things our guests get up to, they really should make us sign confidentiality agreements. I've seen things that would turn that pretty hair white." He shook his head.

"I'm just trying to find out about the woman who walked through the lobby a moment ago. Is she staying here?"

He pursed his lips and tilted his head. "I do have an answer for you, but you need to make it worth my while."

"How about a box of triple chocolate fudge brownies?"

"With candy pop sprinkles and a warm chocolate ganache to dip them into?"

I nodded and smiled. Here was a man who loved his chocolate. "Whatever you want."

He glanced around to check no one was listening. "You have a deal. I can never resist your treats."

"Great. So, the woman? Is she staying here?"

"She is. And she's a haughty madam."

"What's her name?"

"Miss Isabella Northcott. Although the way she behaves, you'd think she was next in line for the throne."

My eyes widened. I'd heard the name Izzie mentioned several times. This must be her. "How long has she been staying?"

"She checked in two days ago."

Which was the same day Lord Rupert's friends arrived at the castle. "Have you seen much of her since she arrived?"

"Unfortunately, I have. She's extremely demanding. We had to change her room three times and then provide fresh out of the packet Egyptian cotton sheets for her bed. All of our linens are the finest quality and get laundered daily, but she didn't believe us. The first room we put her in was on the wrong side of the hotel, the second was too cold, and the third one was simply adequate. If I was in charge of this place, I'd have thrown her out on her bony behind and sent her to the hotel in the next village. She's complained about everything, and she has a terrible temper. I don't think she's given anyone a tip. Mean and tight-fisted. That's not attractive."

"Has she done anything odd while she's been here?"

"Other than be extremely rude to everyone she encounters?"

"I was thinking more about her movements. Has she been out? Or had any visitors?"

"Miss Northcott spends most of her time talking on her phone," he said. "Although the first night she was here, she went out at about nine and didn't return until after two o'clock in the morning. I was on the late shift, bad luck for me. So I saw her leave and return."

"You're sure it was that late?" Those timings fit perfectly for when Kendal was murdered. Izzie could easily have made her way to the castle and seen him.

"Absolutely certain. There's not much else to do other than clock watch on the night shift. But I always have my e-reader with me." He lifted a small black case from his desk. "The boss doesn't mind what we do to keep ourselves awake. I even like to put on a few tunes and dance around the lobby when I feel my eyes getting heavy. She was definitely out doing something she shouldn't late at night. Why the interest in her?"

"Oh! Well, I think she might have visited the castle that night."

"And she put someone's nose out of joint?" He shook his head. "Miss Northcott acts as if she's some high-class lady, but with manners like that, she needs to rethink her role in life."

"Do you have CCTV in the hotel?"

"Of course. It was installed two years ago during the upgrade. Why? You want to have a sneaky look in some guests' rooms?"

"You have cameras in the rooms?"

He chuckled. "Of course not. We have them out the front and the back so we can see everyone coming and going, and we have one tucked up in the corner there so the reception lobby is covered at all times. They're the most vulnerable areas. The boss did it to help bring down the cost of the insurance."

"How long do you keep the recordings for?"

"Thirty days. All these questions. What's going on, Holly Holmes? It sounds like you're investigating something interesting."

I didn't know how widely word had spread yet about what happened to Kendal. I didn't want to be accused of being a gossip, but people would hear about the murder, eventually. "There was an incident at the castle. Somebody died."

John took a step back. "I had no idea. When did this happen?"

"Two days ago. I was just wondering if anyone suspicious had checked into the hotel during that time."

He leaned closer. "You don't think the death was an accident? What are we talking here?"

I bit my lip. "I'd better not say any more. You must keep quiet about it, or no cakes for you."

"You have to tell me more than that. Who was it? What happened to them?"

I backed away. "No! I'll bring the cakes in soon."

"Holly! Don't leave me hanging."

"I'm not. But if I get caught gossiping about what's going on at the castle, I might lose my job."

He huffed out a breath. "Oh, very well. But I want an extra big box of cakes for being kept in the dark about something so juicy."

"I promise, you'll get them." I raced out of the hotel and grabbed the bike.

"Meatball, I think we've just unearthed Kendal's killer."

Chapter 12

"Holly! Watch the oven. The timer's gone off and I don't see you moving," Chef Heston yelled.

I jumped, and raced to the oven, grabbing the oven gloves and pulling the cakes out.

My thoughts had been focused on what I'd learned at the hotel about Izzie Northcott. It couldn't be a coincidence she was here. She had to be involved with this murder.

Chef Heston glowered over my shoulder. "You got lucky that time. Another thirty seconds and they'd have been overdone."

"Sorry, Chef. It won't happen again." I placed the tray of date and pecan muffins on the counter and returned to beating more batter.

"What's wrong with you this afternoon?" he asked. "You've been away with the fairies ever since you returned from the deliveries."

"Oh, you know me. I'm always thinking about food."

"Think about the food you're currently working on, not one of your experimental cake designs." Chef Heston stomped away to yell at somebody else.

I kept my head down and tried to concentrate on the work in hand, but it was hard to do when all I wanted was to find out more about Izzie.

The kitchen was getting quiet as it grew late in the day. The café closed, and the tourists made their way home on their coaches, happy after a long day exploring.

Once the final batch of cakes were out of the oven and cooling on the side, ready for the next day, I took a five-minute break.

I hurried out to Meatball's kennel with a big bowl of food and patted him on the head as he began to eat.

I looked around the quiet garden and took a deep breath. I wasn't sure what my next move should be. Should I tell Campbell about Izzie Northcott and what I'd overheard her talking about? If I did, he might think I was deflecting attention away from myself.

I hadn't seen him since I'd gotten back from my delivery round, which meant he was most likely hard at work figuring out who'd killed Kendal.

The lack of new information on that front worried me. If he hadn't found the real killer yet, his attention could still be on me and my not so excellent alibi.

I returned to the kitchen and studied the crowded white board full of information on the work tasks for each member of the kitchen staff.

My list of tasks was complete. I untied my apron, grabbed two cherry scones, and decided to brave a walk up to the east turret to see Lady Philippa. She'd been the one who'd predicted a death coming to Audley Castle. Maybe she had more insight into what was going on. Even if she didn't, she wouldn't judge me for looking into it.

I ran up the steps two at a time, making sure to ignore the cold spots and what sounded worryingly like a deep male voice telling me to beware. It was only my imagination working overtime. There were no ghosts in the castle. The legends about ghosts were played up for the tourists. There was no such thing as ghosts. Maybe if I told myself that enough times, I'd actually believe it.

"Who's there?" Lady Philippa called as I walked along the wide stone corridor to her rooms.

"It's Holly. I brought you a treat from the kitchen." I pushed open the door, and my mouth dropped open.

She was dressed in a white fluffy unicorn onesie that came with a rainbow tail, a large rainbow colored horn poking out of the back of the hood.

"What do you think? Isn't it fabulous?" She twirled in front of me. "I convinced Alice to lend me her store card. We had a wonderful few hours buying everything you can imagine online. I had no idea you could get such a thing. With the click of a button, everything is ordered and delivered the next day."

I snapped my jaw shut as I walked closer. "Onesies are comfortable. I never had you down as a fan of unicorns, though."

"Everyone's a fan of unicorns. Although the horn isn't all that practical." She flipped the hood up and it almost engulfed her narrow face. "It's such fun. Oooh. Is that for me?" She snagged a cherry scone from my hand.

"What else did you order?" I asked.

"Just you wait and see. This is my first delivery. I've got more coming."

"I can't wait to see it all." If it was anything like the unicorn onesie, I'd be in for a treat.

Lady Philippa stared at me. "What's wrong, girl?"

I let out a sigh as I settled in the seat she pointed at. "Have you heard about Kendal?"

"Of course I have. Alice was telling me all about it. And you discovered the body with her?"

"That's right. And … I'm worried."

She nodded sagely. "I did warn you that death was coming to the castle."

I leaned forward, my scone forgotten. "How did you know?"

Lady Philippa adjusted her tail and took a bite of scone. "Call it a gift, if you like. It's an old family ability."

"To predict the future?"

"It's not so much being able to see what will happen, but it's more like a feeling. I get it in the pit of my stomach. It's like bad indigestion. It stays there until the prediction comes true. Sometimes, I simply have a vague feeling that something bad will happen and keep thinking about particular people."

"You were very specific about a death happening in the castle."

"That's true. But there are other times when I just feel out of sorts. As if I'm coming down with a cold. That's never a good sign. If ever you hear me complaining about having a sniffle, you'll know that trouble isn't far behind."

That still didn't explain how she knew somebody was going to die. "Did you know it would be one of Lord Rupert's friends?"

"No, I'm rarely that exact. If I could predict something bad happening to a specific person, and that does happen now and again, I'd warn them. Well, I'd warn them if I liked them." She ate more scone and chuckled to herself.

"That's quite some ability. You could become famous by making predictions about the future."

Her nose wrinkled, and she plucked the second scone from my hand and took a bite. "I'm famous enough already. Besides, people might fear the family if they learn of this ability. And when you add in the love curse, well, we almost sound like a family of witches."

"Love curse?" This was the first I'd heard about any curse.

"Oh, yes. The Audley family history is riddled with tragedy and troubles. It's all to do with a fourteenth century wise woman who cursed Nicholas Audley. He ordered the woman to be thrown out of her cottage because she was squatting on his land. He threatened to have her killed. In return she cursed him and all future generations of Audleys and anyone related to them, so they would never have a happy ending when it came to love. It's certainly true of my relationship with William."

"But you were happy with your husband, weren't you?"

"Of course! But he died."

"Well, that happens to everyone, eventually. That doesn't mean there was a curse involved. And you're a Carnegie, not an Audley."

"But my daughter married an Audley. That's when the troubles began for us. You should consult Alice's family tree. She's been working on it for months and is always asking questions about some obscure relative. It'll show you the unnatural deaths that have happened. There was Matilda and the husband she lost at sea. Then there was Elizabeth, whose husband died when he was only thirty. Now, we're talking hundreds of years ago, and I realize that disease and poor health were common, but there is always a tragedy linked to a great love in this family. It's because of the wise woman's curse. It needs to be broken. Otherwise, Alice and Rupert will suffer the same fate."

I didn't believe in curses or ghosts, but Lady Philippa seemed so serious. "Is that why Princess Alice is so reluctant about getting married?"

She tipped back her head and laughed. "Of course not. Alice would love to be married; she simply doesn't want to marry any of the weak-willed sycophants her mother keeps pushing on her. She's got a good head on her shoulders, despite trying as hard as possible to convince people she's as daft as a brush. She'll find somebody eventually, fall hopelessly in love, and have her heart broken when he dies tragically because the curse kicks in. I hope you'll be around to comfort her when that happens."

"I really hope it doesn't happen. But of course I'll be here if Princess Alice needs me."

She regarded me shrewdly. "Alice considers you a friend, Holly. Living the lives we do, it's hard to make real friends. You can never be certain who wants to be your friend and who wants to take your money and use your position for their own advantage."

"I'd never do that! I consider Princess Alice a real friend."

"That's good to hear. You have an honest way about you, and I sense a kindness that's often lacking in people. Alice will appreciate you being around when her time of need comes."

I glanced around, not comfortable with how intense the conversation had become. My gaze landed on the binoculars Lady Philippa always kept on the window ledge. "Have you been doing much birdwatching?"

She chuckled. "After a fashion. In fact, I spotted a common blonde socialite creeping around on the night of Kendal's murder. A very common sight. Not at all rare."

My pulse quickened at that news. Could that have been Izzie? "What time did you see her?"

"Around nine o'clock in the evening. I spotted movement outside. A woman approached the castle. She was trying to be stealthy, but I could see her blonde hair tucked under a black hood."

I recalled the night I'd served Lord Rupert and his friends. I'd also seen something outside the castle, just a flash of movement. Could that have been Izzie trying to find a way inside to get to Kendal?

"It was definitely a woman?" I asked.

"Oh yes. Those binoculars are top of the range. Campbell got them for me. She kept her head down, so I couldn't get a good look at her face. She was very small, far too skinny to be healthy, and had long blonde hair that kept sliding out from under the hood. I lost sight of her as she grew close to the castle walls. That's one disadvantage of being up so high. When someone gets near the castle, you can't see what they're doing."

I nodded. That fitted with what John told me. Kendal must have seen Izzie that night. Somehow, she'd gotten into the castle. Maybe Kendal had snuck her in and hidden her in his room so they could have fun together when the party broke up.

"What's on your mind, girl?" Lady Philippa asked. "Do you know who killed Kendal?"

"I'm not certain. I have a few suspects in mind. And there's one person who needs to be at the top of the list."

"Then go and arrest whoever it is. We can't have an unsolved murder on the castle grounds. We've already had enough of those."

That jerked me out of my thoughts. "What do you mean, unsolved murders?"

"Why do you think there are so many ghosts floating around? They're not here for their own entertainment. They have unfinished business. And some of that business involves their murders that were never solved."

"Oh! I don't know about that. I mean, ghosts? Are you sure?"

She leaned forward and patted my hand. "I've been alive a lot longer than you. I've seen it all. Ghosts, curses, and more. They're very real and very much here. We can't help those ghosts, but perhaps you can do something to help with the Kendal issue. The sooner this is cleared up the better."

I worried my bottom lip with my teeth. She was right, and I needed to tell Campbell everything I'd discovered. But if I did that, I'd reveal that I'd been secretly poking around when he'd specifically told me to stay out of this. I doubted many people went against a direct order from Campbell and lived to tell the tale.

I shook my head. I couldn't worry about that. It didn't matter if Campbell was angry with me. The killer had to be stopped, and I was certain it was Izzie Northcott.

"I should go," I said.

"Yes, you should. You've got a mystery to clear up."

I smiled at her. "Thanks for your help."

"You can thank me by getting this matter resolved swiftly and discreetly."

"I'll do my best."

"Those scones were delicious. Thank you. This will be the only meal I'll get tonight. My daughter always forgets me."

I shook my head. That wasn't true. Lady Philippa could dine with everyone else. She simply chose not to and had her meals brought to the turret.

"And you might like to watch yourself on the way out," Lady Philippa called as I hurried along the corridor.

"What do you mean?" I yelped and leaped backward, slamming against the cold stone wall as a looming figure stepped out of the shadows.

Laughter drifted through the open door. "I warned you."

"Oh my word!" My hand pressed over my racing heart. "Campbell! Don't do that! I nearly died of fright."

His eyes narrowed, and he shook his head. "We need to talk, Miss Holmes."

I lifted my chin and nodded. "Yes, we do."

Chapter 13

My stomach fluttered with nerves as I walked ahead of Campbell to the kitchen. I'd resolved to speak to him about what I'd discovered, but he'd gotten the jump on me. Now it would look like I'd been hiding things.

"Cup of tea?" I asked as we reached the kitchen. I was grateful to find it quiet.

"No. What are you playing at?"

I took a deep breath and turned toward him. "I'm not playing. I'm trying to help."

"Helping by interfering with a murder investigation."

"I haven't interfered."

"You were seen questioning Izzie Northcott in the village today."

I gulped. "That was by accident. I overheard her talking on her phone about Kendal. I thought it might be useful to see what she knew."

"And was it an accident that you followed her to the hotel?"

"Oh! Well, no. I was just curious about her."

"And then you proceeded to ask the desk clerk, completely by accident I'm guessing, everything he knew about her and if there was any CCTV in the hotel?"

Oops! I'd been well and truly found out. "Have you got someone following me?"

"It's my responsibility to keep the residents of this castle safe."

"Does that include keeping me safe?"

"No, but you are a suspect in a murder investigation, and therefore you need to be scrutinized."

"Are you still doubting my alibi?"

He glared at me for a long uncomfortable second. "I no longer consider you a suspect. But you are ringing alarm bells by poking around in this murder."

"I wasn't doing it to cause trouble. And I was just about to tell you what I'd discovered, after I'd spoken to Lady Philippa."

"Why bother her with this matter?"

"I thought she might help me gain a new perspective on what I'd learned."

"I'm sure she did. When she's not filling your head with misinformation about family curses."

"I don't believe in curses. And you shouldn't be eavesdropping on a private conversation."

"I'll eavesdrop on any conversation I care to if it helps to solve a murder." He stared at me without blinking. "What happened to my cakes?"

My forehead wrinkled. "What are you talking about?"

"Weren't you making me cakes so you could sweeten me up?"

Was there no secret I could keep from Campbell? "I wasn't exactly trying to sweeten you up."

"So, it was a straightforward bribe?"

"No! I had no reason to bribe you."

"At the time, you were considered a suspect in this murder."

I sighed. "Maybe I did think the cakes would make you warm to me. I know I'm innocent, but by the way you glared at me every time we met, you considered me trouble."

"I still do consider you trouble. So, what happened to the cakes?"

"They went to a much better cause. The gardeners ate them. They've done amazing work on their herb memorial garden. I figured they deserved them."

"Do you consider the work I do not amazing?"

I snorted out a laugh. "I'm sure you always get a gold star from the Duke every time he does your appraisal."

A smirk slid across his face. "The Duke doesn't do my appraisals."

"The Duchess?"

He arched an eyebrow. "Let's just say my appraisals take place off site."

"Let me guess, at a top-secret location run by some dark shadowy force who oversees the safety of the entire planet."

He shrugged. "You're not far off the mark."

"And do they give you gold stars for your work?"

"Several. Since you've been snooping around, you'd better tell me everything you've learned."

"You probably already know everything," I said.

"Tell me in your own words. Leave nothing out."

"That's exactly what I'd planned to do. I haven't been doing this for any underhand reason."

"Good to hear. I'm still waiting."

I huffed out a breath. "Okay. I was in the village making my last delivery of cakes. I'd just stopped for a breather before coming back to the castle, when I overheard a posh woman on her phone talking about Kendal's death."

"What did she say?"

"It sounded like she wasn't bothered about what happened to him. All she cared about was having to find new guys to fill her social calendar. She caught me listening and asked me what I was doing. I got the impression she thought I was a celebrity hunter or looking to have my photograph taken with her."

"You do know who Izzie Northcott is?"

"All I know about her is that she's rude and thinks she's better than everybody else."

"Her father set up Kitten Cosmetics. Well, actually, his first wife did, but he took all the credit and divorced her."

"Kitten Cosmetics! Don't they produce makeup that's supposed to make you look ten years younger?"

"I've never tried it. It's made the family a fortune."

"Does Izzie work for the company?"

"She has a full-time job as a socialite. No wonder she's annoyed about Kendal's death. According to the gossip magazines, he can't take a bad picture."

"You read the gossip magazines?"

He clicked his tongue. "Continue. What else did Izzie say?"

"She wouldn't tell me who she was, so I followed her to the hotel and … discovered her identity for myself." I needed to be careful about how much I said. I wasn't dropping John in it for sharing information with me.

"You mean you bribed the desk clerk?" He raised a hand. "Don't even try to deny it. We've already been at the hotel. John has told us everything. He said you were very persuasive. Something about triple chocolate fudge brownies?"

I shrugged. "Cakes are my secret weapon."

Campbell's gaze landed on a container of chocolate flapjacks on the kitchen counter. "Don't I know it? What did he tell you about Miss Northcott?"

"That she was rude and ungrateful. Most importantly, he told me that she left the hotel during the exact time window when Kendal was murdered."

"And how do you know exactly when he was killed, if you had nothing to do with it?"

Again, I needed to be careful not to get my sources in any trouble. "Somebody told me the time of his death. Which I found particularly helpful since you weren't sharing."

"It's not my job to help you. And at the time, I was withholding information because you were a suspect."

"But you're willing to share with me now?"

His nostrils flared. "What else?"

"I can't be certain, but the night Kendal was killed, I saw someone outside the castle."

"You reported this to my security team?"

"No. I thought it was one of your security team. It was a brief flash of movement outside one of the downstairs windows. I assumed it was someone patrolling outside. That was until I'd spoken to Lady Philippa. She also saw someone outside at the same time. It was a woman with blonde hair. Izzie has blonde hair."

"That doesn't mean it was her. There are lots of blonde women, and Kendal had a particular liking for blondes. Was Lady Philippa able to give a positive identification?"

"No, all she saw was a skinny, blonde woman."

"What were your impressions of Miss Northcott when you met?"

"I didn't get a single positive vibe off her. She was cold, unfriendly, and thought the world owed her."

"She was mean to you?"

"She may have said Meatball looked flea-bitten, and I was a sweaty mess."

He chuckled. "Anything else?"

"That's just about it." I looked away. "Although I did hear that Kendal may have entertained someone in his room the night he died."

"Did you now? It appears there are leaks all over the castle," he said.

"Is that true? Was he with someone that evening?"

"It's being looked into. Would you place money on it being Miss Northcott who was in the room with Kendal?"

"I don't gamble, but if I did, then yes. I think she came to Audley St. Mary specifically to see Kendal. She even said they might get married in the future. Maybe she was worried he might be cheating on her so came to see what he was up to. Or Kendal invited her and snuck her in, I don't know. Maybe they fought while she was here."

"She killed him in the castle and took the body outside?"

"No. She's really tiny. Izzie couldn't carry a body. Maybe he escorted her out, and she lured him into the woods. She could have used her feminine wiles."

"They can be deadly."

"It's possible Izzie convinced Kendal to go with her and then struck him, panicked, and buried the body. And, when we met, I noticed she was missing a false nail. She could have lost that when she dug the hole. You should look for that."

Campbell stared at me in silence.

"What? Am I in trouble?"

"Have you thought of a career as a spy?"

A surprised laugh shot out of me. "Are you kidding?"

"I never kid. You're good at noticing the little details. That's an excellent spy trait."

I couldn't help but feel flattered. Most people would simply call me nosy or tell me to mind my own business, just like Izzie.

"Tell me what life is like as a spy," I said.

"How should I know?"

"Well, you're a spy."

"I'm not a spy."

"You've worked undercover."

"Have I?"

"I know you have."

"And you know that how? You've read my confidential files?"

I tutted. "No. But you wouldn't be here if you weren't great at what you did."

"Of course I'm great at what I do."

I opened the container of chocolate flapjacks. "Would you like a piece?"

"Bribery doesn't work on me. And believe me, I've been offered plenty of bribes during my service to this country."

"Ah! But has anyone bribed you with flapjacks covered in a rich Belgian chocolate and infused with apricot brandy?" I lifted a piece and held it out to him.

His eyes glittered and his lips curled up. "Tread carefully, Holly Holmes. You really don't want to mess with me."

"Who's messing? I'm simply offering you something nice to eat."

The kitchen door slammed open. Lord Rupert blundered in, skidding to a halt as he saw me with Campbell. "Oh! I didn't know you had company."

I lowered the flapjack and placed it back in the container. "It's not a problem. How may I help you, Lord Rupert?"

His worried gaze shot to Campbell before he looked at me. "Are you on a … a date?"

Campbell pulled his shoulders back and clasped his hands in front of him. "No, sir. I'm on duty."

"This isn't a date," I said hurriedly. "We were just … talking." I couldn't exactly tell Rupert that we'd been discussing his friend's murder.

"Oh! My mistake. Still, I didn't mean to get in the way. I should leave." Rupert turned and raced out of the kitchen before I had a chance to stop him.

I sighed. I didn't want him getting the wrong idea about Campbell and me. I mean, Campbell was gorgeous, but he was terrifying. If I got on the wrong side of him, he'd simply make me disappear one dark and scary night. And I expect he had all sorts of twisted skeletons lurking in his closet, probably some of them ex-girlfriends. I didn't want to become one of them.

"That's another thing you need to be careful of," Campbell said.

"What's that?" I tore my gaze from the closed door.

"Lord Rupert. We can't have Holly the Superspy getting too attached to her employer. I might have to start calling you Lady Holly Holmes. That really sticks in the throat."

I gulped. "It's not like that. We're just—"

"Friends?"

"Exactly. Lord Rupert's a sweet man."

"You have a knack for wheedling your way in with this family. Are you sure you haven't been trained in the fine arts of seduction?"

"Seduction! No! I mean, I wouldn't know how to seduce. I don't do that. I'm … I'm not even in a relationship. I've been single for ages. I don't even know how to flirt. I get clumsy around a man I like. I … I mean, no. I'm not a wheedler."

He lifted a hand and chuckled. "Yes, as you've just ably demonstrated, seduction isn't your strong point. Although your food has a certain seductive quality to it."

My cheeks felt like they were on fire. "Are you suggesting that I'm seducing Lord Rupert by giving him cake?"

"There are worse ways to seduce a man. The way to a man's heart is through his stomach. And you always know how to give people what they want when they're looking for the perfect dessert."

"Does that mean you don't want the flapjack? You don't want to risk being tempted by my flapjacks and spill your darkest secrets to me."

"Did you make them?"

"If I say yes, will you think I'm trying to seduce you?"

He grabbed a flapjack out of the container and took a large bite. He thumped his chest with a fist. "It's official. I've just lost my heart to you."

"Very funny. I assure you, there's nothing going on between Lord Rupert and me. Although he did look surprised when he saw us talking. You don't think …" It was too ridiculous to contemplate. He was a lord. There could never be anything between us. Rupert couldn't like me.

"If I tell you what I think, will you pay any attention to me?"

"I might. But I don't want to hurt Lord Rupert's feelings."

"Then maybe you should quit your job."

"Quit! I love it here."

"Then back off. Back off from your investigation of this murder and back off from being so friendly with your employers, especially Lord Rupert. As you say, he's a good guy."

"I don't mean to give people the wrong impression about me. I'm just—"

"Yes, I get it. You're just friendly. You find out what people love and you make it for them. Some would call that manipulative."

"And some would call it simply being a nice person." I crossed my arms over my chest. "Which I am. If you don't like it, you can stop eating my flapjacks and leave this kitchen."

He finished the flapjack and grinned. "I'm not going anywhere."

"And neither am I. And I'll be friends with whoever I want to."

"Just keep it as friends."

"You might be in charge of the safety of the Audleys, but you're not in charge of me or who I choose to make as a friend."

He leaned back against the kitchen counter and shoved his hands in his pants pockets. "If I think your friendship with any of them puts them at risk, it will come to an end."

"What are you going to do, tell them I'm a security threat? Suggest they fire me?"

He arched an eyebrow. "I have much simpler ways of making a person stop doing something I don't want them to do."

I lifted the container of flapjacks, my hands only shaking slightly as I shoved them in the chiller, away from Campbell. No more treats for him.

"Anyway, you don't need to chase potential suspects anymore," Campbell said. "Izzie Northcott is being formally questioned about her involvement with Kendal and where she was when he was murdered. All the evidence points to her."

I turned back to him. "Are you sure?"

"As sure as twenty years of dedicated service to this country will allow me to be. Do you think otherwise?"

"Izzie's a good suspect. I suppose if things went wrong between them and Kendal rejected her, she would do something about it."

"A woman scorned is a deadly thing."

"How would you know? Have you ever been married?"

I only got a smirk in response to those questions.

"When a person's in love and gets rejected," I said, "it can send them crazy. Maybe Izzie is the person you're looking for. But what about the others? Have you ruled them all out?"

"Who are you referring to?" Campbell asked.

"Kendal's other friends. Chris, Simon, and Anthony. They were all here that night, and they'd arranged to go shooting together the next day. What if something happened?"

"You think they all got together and shot Kendal?"

"No. I know he wasn't shot."

Campbell sighed. "Not only have you found out the time of Kendal's murder, you also know what the murder weapon was."

"Um, not exactly. Maybe that was a lucky guess." I rubbed my forehead. I needed to be more discreet if I was to continue investigating this murder.

"Holly, this has to stop now. We've got a person of interest in custody, and we've spoken to everyone else."

"You know where everyone else was when Kendal was killed? You have no doubts?"

He leaned forward. "Trust me, I know everything. This case is over. No more questions." He turned and left the kitchen.

I shook my head, unease running through me. Campbell might think he had all the answers, but I wasn't so sure.

There were loose ends to tie up. Until they were sorted, I wouldn't be satisfied.

Chapter 14

"Two more miles and we'll be home," I puffed as I leaned over the front of the basket.

Meatball stood and licked the underside of my chin.

I laughed as we reached the top of the hill and coasted down it. I remembered the last time I'd done that and made sure to keep my feet on the pedals and my hand lightly pressing the brake. I'd be in complete control just in case I ran into anybody I shouldn't.

The bike felt heavy and began to slow even though we were going downhill. I took my hand off the brake, but it didn't help.

Metal scraped against the ground, and I groaned. "Just what we need." I pulled the bike over to the side of the road and hopped off. As I'd feared, the front tire was flat.

"We could do without this, Meatball. I'm starving. It's time for our lunch."

"Woof, woof." He wagged his tail.

I stared at the tire for a second, silently willing it to inflate and get us home.

"Woof?" Meatball peered over the edge of the basket.

"No miracle is going to happen this time. We'll have to fix this ourselves." It wouldn't be the first time I'd changed a bike tire, and I always kept a puncture repair kit in the basket with Meatball for just this eventuality.

I lifted the cushion he sat on and had just eased out the repair kit when a car zoomed up beside me and screeched to a halt.

"Hey! It's the cake lady." Christian sat behind the wheel of a sleek shiny red Ferrari.

"Hello. Are you going somewhere nice?" I asked.

"Just meeting the others at the pub for a quick drink. Problem with your bike?" He leaned over and stared at it.

"A flat tire."

"Do you need a hand getting it fixed?"

I glanced at him. I knew exactly how to fix the bike, but this gave me an opportunity to talk about Kendal. "Yes, please. I don't know what I'm doing. I could really do with some help." If I was a mistress of seduction, this would be where I'd flutter my lashes and pout, but I'd told Campbell the truth yesterday: I was terrible at flirting.

"Give me two seconds." Christian maneuvered the car to the side of the road and shut off the engine before hopping out. He was dressed in a tight-fitting green polo shirt and smart dark jeans.

I couldn't help but notice he had an impressive physique under those clothes.

"Let's take a look." Christian leaned over the bike. "This thing is ancient. Where are your gears?"

"Oh, well, we do things the old-fashioned way at the castle. My boss thinks it's charming to offer a bike delivery service."

"I bet he doesn't ride this old thing. It's an antique."

I laughed. "Not a chance."

Christian dinged the bell on the front of the handlebars. "My racer's got fifteen gears."

"You like to cycle?"

"Of course. Keeping fit's my thing, in case you hadn't noticed." He flexed his biceps. "Not bad, huh?"

My cheeks flushed, and I looked away. "I can see you take care of yourself."

"I have to. I'm head of a fitness company. We mainly sell protein drinks, energy bars, that sort of thing, but we're diversifying into sporting equipment, including bikes."

It made sense now why he looked so buff.

Christian stared at the bike for several seconds before scratching his chin. He squeezed the flat tire in several places. "It's been a while since I've changed a bike tire. Still, it must be just like riding a bike, eh? You never forget the basics."

"I'm sure you're right," I said. "Did you ever go biking with Kendal?"

"Ha! Kendal wasn't into fitness. His idea of a workout was lifting a pint of ale off the bar. The guy was getting sloppy as he got older. You know what it's like. When you're young, your body can take punishment and you bounce right back. You can go out on an all-night drinking session and wake up with nothing more than a slight headache the next morning. Not anymore. Kendal tried to deny it, but the drink was getting the best of him."

"He had a problem with alcohol?"

"Not so much. He wasn't an alcoholic, but he always thought he was more fun when he had a drink in his hand. I preferred the old Kendal. Although that version of him was no angel. The guy he turned into was exactly the sort of person you expected to wind up murdered in the woods."

That was a blunt statement. "Why do you say that?"

Christian stood from his inspection of the bike. "Because Kendal was a cheat, a jerk, and a liar."

"You sound like you hated him."

He tipped back on his heels. "Even when he was young, Kendal could be annoying. He got himself the label of class clown at school and was always joking around and making fun of everybody else. Sometimes it could be funny, but it was often spiteful. He could get mean and make things personal. And he used to wind up Rupert all the time. That didn't stop when we left school. It was like he'd stuck a target on Rupert's back and was always going for him."

"What sort of things did he do?" My heart clenched in sympathy for Rupert.

"Sometimes it was just dumb stuff, like hiding his textbooks or messing up his homework. Now and again, it would get dark and we'd have to have a word and tell him to back off. On one occasion, he locked Rupert in a closet all night. He dragged him into an empty room and trapped him in there. Rupert was humiliated. He tried to fight back, but Kendal knew how to use his fists. Rupert ended up with a bloody nose and a black eye. He tried to laugh it off, but you could see it hurt the guy. Why wouldn't it?"

"Yet Rupert remained friends with Kendal? If someone did that to me, I wouldn't speak to them ever again." I jammed my hands on my hips. If Kendal wasn't already dead, I'd be having words with him. Nobody liked a bully.

"Lucky for you, your parents don't hang out in the same social circles as ours. It's expected. We're supposed to get along together just like our dads did when they went to Eton. It's a bit sad, really. I tolerated Kendal because I had no other option. Rupert was the same."

I shook my head, my insides boiling with anger. Rupert rarely talked about his time at school, and I was beginning to understand why. It sounded like it had been a miserable time in his life.

"Thinking about it now, Rupert even missed a whole term. His parents told the school that he had glandular fever, but I reckon it was because he was stressed. It wasn't long after the whole getting locked in the closet incident with Kendal."

"I can see now why somebody might want Kendal dead," I huffed out.

Christian shrugged. "Which is why I wasn't surprised by what happened to him. He was a joker right until the end."

"He played a trick on you when you were here?"

Christian nodded. "The night before we went clay pigeon shooting, Rupert took us to the gun room. We were checking over the shotguns, making sure the balance and sighting was right. I turned my back for five minutes, only to discover that Kendal was messing with my gun."

"What was he doing to it?"

"I wasn't sure. It looked like he was trying to shove something into one of the barrels. It could have jammed and taken my hand off when I pulled the trigger." He shook his head. "Of course, he swore he wasn't doing that and was just taking a look to see if my gun was better than his. I didn't believe him. The guy was an idiot. He never thought through the consequences of his actions."

I studied Christian as he bent over my bicycle wheel again and tried to tug off the rubber. Here was a motive for wanting Kendal dead. Christian had caught him trying to damage his gun, which would have injured him. He'd finally had enough of Kendal playing the fool. It sounded like there was no love lost between them. Had Christian seen an opportunity to get rid of Kendal once and for all and acted on it?

"Have you been questioned about what happened to Kendal?" I asked.

He shrugged as he focused on the bike. "Sure. The scary guy in the suit asked me where I was. I had no worries about answering his questions. Simon's my alibi. That night, we'd all had a lot to drink. In fact, I barely remember the evening. Rupert's always so generous when it comes to entertaining. He got in our favorite drinks and we went to town on them, knocking back doubles. And of course, there were your delicious cakes to enjoy. Even so, I got the munchies, so headed off with Simon and raided your kitchen." He grinned at me. "I hope you don't mind. There were all sorts of delicious leftovers in the fridge."

"That's what it's there for." I needed to check with Chef Heston to see if any food had gone missing from the fridge that night. Given how drunk Simon and Christian would have been, they'd have left behind a trail of devastation.

Christian stepped back from the bike and shook his head. "Anyway, that whole mess is sorted now. The police have Kendal's crazy ex in custody."

"Crazy ex? You mean Izzie?"

"The very girl. Kendal used to call her his sexy stalker. We've known Izzie for years. She was always hanging around with us even when we were teenagers. She got herself a reputation for being a wild child. Kendal adored the wild women. He said it was something about how forbidden they were. He loved to enjoy himself with the kind of woman he'd never take home to his parents."

"Izzie wasn't marriage material?"

"I can't imagine anyone would want to marry Izzie Northcott. She's a beautiful girl, and a heck of a lot of fun to be with, but once you get a reputation like that in our circles, it's hard to get rid of. Kendal had his fun and then told her it was over. She wasn't buying it. She really did stalk him. It got intense between them."

"Did Kendal make Izzie think she stood a chance with him?"

He grinned. "Most likely. I suspect Kendal promises the women he entertains a lot of things. He even joked once that he told Izzie he'd marry her. The foolish girl actually believed him. He said that she'd turned up at his apartment and was screaming outside the window when she learned the truth. In the end, he called the police and had her taken away. I could never see Kendal settling with one woman. He was always a ladies' man."

"He was seeing other women as well as Izzie?"

"You can guarantee it. That only made Izzie crazier. She wanted Kendal to herself. She was so deluded. In the end, I felt sorry for her. He pushed her too far. This is the end result. She tracked Kendal here and killed him. I expect there are more than a few people happy with her actions. It's just a pity she got caught. She was jolly good fun on the party scene."

That was another nail in the coffin in regard to Izzie's guilt. A big part of me didn't blame her if she had killed Kendal. He'd led her on and used her to get what he wanted, then thrown her away like she meant nothing to him. The more I learned about Kendal Jakes, the less I liked him.

"I've been beaten." Christian stepped back. "This bike has bested me. It's these old models, you see. And it's been a while since I've had to fix my own bike."

"Tires are tricky to fix." I'd have had that tire off, patched up, and inflated by now.

"You bet they are." He checked his watch. "I need to get a move on or I'll be late to meet the guys."

"Oh! Well, thanks for trying."

"Sure. Nice chatting with you." Christian hopped into his car and zoomed off.

I shook my head as I looked at Meatball. "One day, I'll meet a guy who can add value to our lives."

"Woof."

"Maybe you're right. We add enough value to our own lives." I knelt, removed the flat tire, and made the patch repair to the wheel before using the hand pump to inflate it so it would get us home.

Maybe there really was no more mystery to solve. The police had the right person. Izzie fit the profile perfectly. A beautiful woman, neglected by the man she loved. She'd turned into a stalker, obsessed with her ex, and had taken things too far.

A tiny flicker of doubt niggled in my mind. I just needed to cover all the bases and make sure the police had the right person.

Izzie Northcott had been through enough when it came to Kendal. I had to be a hundred percent sure she was guilty.

Chapter 15

Yesterday had been a crazily busy day. I'd only been back at the castle for ten minutes before five unexpected coachloads of tourists arrived all demanding refreshments.

I'd had no time to think about the murder when I was elbow deep in making cakes and huge mounds of sandwiches to feed the hungry hordes.

Despite sliding into bed at midnight, I was up early.

My weighted hula hoop had arrived yesterday. Although I kept fit on the bike, I could never resist a fitness trend. I'd tried them all: weighted vests for running in, hot yoga, resistance bands, a balancing board where you stood on one leg to help strengthen your core.

Given the early hour, no one else was about. I hurried outside in my exercise gear: lycra leggings covered in baggy shorts, a supportive bra, and an oversized T-shirt. Meatball was by my side, delighted to be out so early.

I picked my favorite secluded spot, just past the rose gardens where the compost heaps sat away from public view. I always came here when I wanted to exercise. It wasn't overlooked by anyone in the castle, and visitors rarely came here. The compost heap got pretty pungent on a hot day.

"Okay, Meatball. Let's see how this thing works." I unrolled the instructions for the hula hoop and began to read.

"Woof woof." He made a grab for the hoop.

"Noooo! This isn't for you." I pointed to the instructions. "It says here that the hoop helps to burn calories, build strength, and reduce belly fat."

"Woof."

"It's true." I squeezed my lower belly. "I'm getting an actual muffin top. The only muffins I want to see are those I pull from the oven." I gave the hoop an experimental swing around my hips. It fell to the ground.

I kept reading. "Hoops were used by the ancient Greeks and Egyptians. How interesting. They got a lot of things right. Fun exercise equipment being one of them."

"Woof." Meatball jumped at the hoop again. He clearly thought it was an oversized dog toy bought specifically for his entertainment and not my waistline.

I grabbed a chewy bone-shaped toy from my pocket and slung it. "Go fetch."

Meatball raced off after the toy, his tail wagging.

"Ooh, even better. This burns as many calories as kickboxing. Wow! Four hundred calories." I flipped over the information sheet. "Oh! In an hour." I didn't want to have to gyrate for an hour. I might pop a hip! Still, if I could do it, that was one more triple chocolate muffin I could enjoy with no consequences.

It was time to get my hoop on. I swung the hoop to get it going and thrust my hips. It fell to the ground before I could get momentum.

I tried several more times. This thing was heavy, and it was hitting my hip bones. If I wasn't careful, I'd get bruises.

This was harder than it looked. I was okay with a lightweight plastic hula hoop, but the added weight of this hoop made it almost impossible.

I wasn't giving up. I kept thrusting my hips backward and forward, trying to keep the hoop up, but kept failing.

"I must be missing a trick," I muttered.

I tried again and yelped as Meatball launched in the air and grabbed the edge of the hula hoop.

"Hey! Paws off my hoop."

Meatball dropped to the ground, but his gaze was focused, ready to pounce at the next opportunity.

I held up a finger and used my sternest voice. "No! This isn't for you. Go explore the garden while I exercise."

I tried another rotation of the hula hoop, but with the extra weight and Meatball jumping up and down trying to grab the hoop, this wasn't going so well.

Laughter drifted toward me. I grabbed the hula hoop and looked around swiftly.

Simon was leaning against a tree, watching me, amusement dancing in his eyes.

"Oh! I didn't think anybody else would be up so early." Heat traveled up my neck. How long had he been standing there?

"You've almost got it." He pushed away from the tree with a casual ease. "I can show you how it's done if you like."

My eyes widened as I passed him the hula hoop. "How do you know how to use a hoop?"

He grinned as he slid it over his head and secured it around his waist. "I have five sisters."

I watched, more than a little jealous as he expertly twirled the hula hoop. Even Meatball was impressed as he sat and watched the hoop.

"It's all in the movement of the hips. With the extra weight, you have to thrust backward and forward that bit faster." His movements looked a little obscene, but I studied them anyway, eager to learn how to conquer the hoop. "All you're lacking is the speed."

"Thanks for showing me how it's done." I took the hoop back.

"No worries. Give it a go."

"I'm done for the day." I had no plans to thrust like that in front of Simon at any point in the next one hundred years.

"My sisters went through a hula hoop obsession one summer. They all had them. They'd spend hours practicing with their hoops. They insisted I take part. I hated it at the time, but it helped me gain a rhythm that most guys my age seriously lacked. The ladies sure appreciate it." He winked at me.

"Five sisters must be a challenge. Are you the only boy in your family?"

"Sadly, yes. My parents always wanted a boy. They kept getting girls. I was the last one to arrive, and now have five older, bossy, annoying sisters." He leaned closer. "Don't tell anybody this, but they sometimes dressed me up like a doll. I'm scarred for life by those girls."

I grinned. I hadn't had much to do with Simon so far, but he seemed nice. "I won't tell a soul."

"I like to think having so many sisters gave me an edge over my clumsy friends. Some of them had no experience of being around the fairer sex, and there was rarely the chance to do so when we were at school. I knew all about girls. I understood that they loved to talk and share their feelings. That was what I was used to. It was a massive shock when I went to an all boys' school and all they wanted to talk about was sports, food, and breaking wind."

"How did Kendal get on at school?"

"Ah, yes. Everyone's talking about him," Simon said with a shrug. "He got on just fine. He used to joke around and make people laugh. That made him popular."

"I spoke to Christian yesterday. He said they have Izzie Northcott in custody for Kendal's murder."

"I know. I don't understand it. It seems so unlikely that she'd have killed him."

"What makes you say that?" I asked.

He took the hula hoop back and swirled it around his arm. "I told the guy who's been interviewing us, Campbell something or other, that I saw someone outside the castle the night Kendal was killed."

"Who was it?"

"I didn't get a good look. I got this weird feeling we were being watched when we were in the games room. I looked out the window a few times but didn't see anyone. Then all of a sudden, somebody dashed past."

"Was it one of the other guys? Maybe somebody playing a prank on you, trying to bring the ghost rumors to life?"

He smiled. "No, it wasn't any of us. We were all together most of the evening."

"Do you think Izzie was watching you?"

"Why didn't she just come inside if it was her? We were all friends. I've always liked Izzie. She's a sweet girl. The reputation she has isn't deserved."

"What reputation does she have?" I already knew the answer but was interested in Simon's take on Izzie.

He raised his eyebrows. "Not a great one. But we all make mistakes when we're young. She's changed now she's older. I used to date Izzie before Kendal pinched her off me."

"He stole your girlfriend?"

"We weren't exclusive, but it didn't feel great to know she preferred him to me."

Could Simon have been jealous of Izzie's relationship with Kendal? Had he decided to kill the competition so he could get back together with her?

"You must have been jealous," I said.

He looked at the ground. "I was probably more serious about things than she was. Izzie loves to party. I'm not against it, but it needs to be with the right people in the right place. I won't go to any old party just to be seen. Besides, my work keeps me busy. I'm in IT if you didn't know. I've got offices all around the world, and they're always contacting me at weird times of the night with some problem. If I was drinking and partying all the time, I'd miss something important. I tried to explain that to Izzie, but she didn't understand. Then I lost the chance to make a go of things with her. Kendal wowed her with his party lifestyle. That was it. Game over for us."

"Maybe you can comfort Izzie now. She must need a friend."

His lips pursed before he shook his head. "I'm not so sure about that. I like the girl, but I don't want to date a criminal."

"You're convinced she's guilty?"

"I mean, the police are, as is Campbell. I just, I don't know …"

"Other than the person outside the castle that night, did you see anything else unusual?"

"Not a thing. We were in the games room drinking way too much. I headed off with Christian to the kitchen to grab some carbs and soak up the booze. It was a typical night with these guys."

"And you don't think any of your other friends had a problem with Kendal? I've heard a rumor or two that his jokes could be at the expense of others."

He scrubbed at his chin. "True enough. Kendal lived for the moment. He didn't care about the consequences of his actions, so long as everyone laughed with him. I mean, it could hack you off, but you get used to it. Although Tony's not been a fan of Kendal's for a while."

"Tony?"

"Yes, you met him the other night. Anthony Bambridge. We call him Tony. Anyway, he had a real beef with Kendal. He lost him a lot of money."

"How did that happen?"

"Tony foolishly invested in one of Kendal's companies. Kendal spent all the money on equipment and marketing and was completely off target. He lost the lot, and Tony didn't get a penny of his investment back. I always thought it would be Tony who would wring Kendal's neck, not Izzie. It's a shame if she did it. I liked her."

"Holly! I expect to see you in the kitchen in twenty minutes." Chef Heston strode past, his car keys dangling from his fingers. "We've got a busy day today."

I checked the time and gasped. I'd been out here longer than I'd realized and hadn't had breakfast or showered yet. "Thanks, Simon. I appreciate the hula hoop lesson."

He grinned. "Any time. But remember, this is our little secret. I'm all man, not some hula hoop loving geek who secretly enjoys being dressed up by my sisters."

I laughed as I hurried away with Meatball, the hula hoop clamped under my arm. This was useful new information. Simon must have been annoyed about Kendal stealing Izzie from him, but he had a decent alibi. However, Tony hated Kendal because he'd lost him money.

Campbell must have investigated this and discounted it, but I still wanted to make sure the police had the right person.

I had to find a way to speak to Tony and figure out just how angry he'd been with Kendal. If he was angry enough to kill, I might have a new suspect on my hands.

Chapter 16

I took a five-minute shower before dressing and dashing to the kitchen with my hair still damp. I had two minutes to get to work before I was late.

"Stop right there by orders of the Princess." Alice giggled as she stepped out from behind a bush. "Where are you going in such a hurry?"

Meatball bounded over to Alice, and she scooped him up and rained pink lipstick kisses all over his head.

"Work! I got distracted this morning. Chef Heston will only yell if I'm late."

"I'll come with you." Alice set Meatball down, grabbed my elbow, and tucked a hand through it. "I've been meaning to catch up with you. Have you heard the latest on the murder investigation?"

"Campbell thinks that Izzie Northcott did it."

She giggled again. "Then you don't know the absolute latest."

I slowed and looked at her. "They've let Izzie go?"

"The exact opposite. She's been charged with Kendal's murder."

"Wow! That was quick work. So they've got no doubts about her being guilty?"

"Of course not. Campbell's in charge and he's so good at what he does." Alice sighed. "Don't you think he's terribly handsome?"

I stopped walking before I reached the entrance to the kitchen and turned to her. "You have the hots for Campbell?"

She slapped me on the arm. "I never said that."

"You don't have to. Your blushing is giving you away." Was she being serious? This had to be a crush. The princess and the bodyguard? It sounded like something straight out of a Hallmark movie.

"I'm not blushing. It's just hot out here." She fanned her face with her hand. "Don't you think he's ever so dashing? And he looks so good in those suits he wears. Imagine what he'd look like in a tuxedo?"

"Alice! What will your mom think if you fall for the bodyguard?"

"Mommy's not even around to notice." She pressed a finger to her lips. "You mustn't say a word. It's our secret. In fact, I'm ordering you to be silent, or I'll have your head chopped off."

Yikes! I sometimes wondered just how serious Alice was with her threats of putting people in the tower and having their heads lopped off.

She smacked me on the arm again. "Only joking! I'd need a jolly good reason for having your head chopped off. Although I'm sure I can come up with one if I think hard enough."

"That's very kind of you," I muttered.

She laughed out loud. "I'm just relieved this horrible business is all over. So is Rupert. The poor chap has never been able to handle stress. I was just thinking, he needs some of your magic muffins to make him happy again."

"There's nothing magic about my muffins." I turned, and we continued our walk to the kitchen.

"Rupert thinks there is. He's always going on about how great you are, and how amazing your food is."

I felt a little smug and happy about that. It was always nice when someone praised your work.

"I'll make something special today if I get the chance. I've been working on an old recipe I discovered. I haven't cracked it yet, but I've got a new ingredient to add."

"Oh! He loves your experiments," Alice said. "Remember when you made those medieval fig tarts? They had strange spices in them."

"Saffron, cinnamon, mace, peppers, and cloves. I wasn't sure they were that big a hit. Most people are used to super sweet desserts. Anything that doesn't have a ton of sugar in it is usually rejected."

"Rupert loved them. You could probably serve him a bowl of plain cornflakes and milk and he'd tell you that you were a genius. My brother's very ... fond of you."

"I like him too." I looked away. Maybe I liked Lord Rupert a little too much, but I'd drawn a line when it came to our relationship. We were simply friends. There was nothing more to it.

Chef Heston yanked open the kitchen door as I approached, and his eyes narrowed. He opened his mouth as if to yell but spotted Alice and snapped it shut. "Time to get to work, Miss Holmes."

"Good luck," Alice whispered as she kissed my cheek and hurried away.

I let out a sigh as I headed into the kitchen and grabbed my apron. This mystery really had been solved. Everyone thought Izzie had killed Kendal. Maybe I should too. I was worrying about nothing.

"This had better be right," I muttered under my breath as I looked critically at the solid lump of Roman honey bread cooling on the tray.

I'd tried a dozen different versions of this recipe and they either turned out too stodgy, flat, or as hard as a rock.

"What have you got there?" Chef Heston stomped over and glared at the honey bread.

"Before you yell at me, all my tasks are done for the day and everything's tidied up. I made this on my own time using ingredients I paid for."

He snorted and peered at my creation. "So, what is it?"

"I'm re-creating some ancient recipes I found in an old book. This is Roman honey bread."

He lowered his head and sniffed. "You've got a lot of spices in there. It could be overpowering to the palate."

"I followed the recipe. Although I adjusted the amount of liquid and added extra honey. My last few attempts haven't come out right."

"Get me a knife." He held his hand out.

I did as instructed, and he eased the knife into the bread before sliding it out.

"Comes out clean. Evenly cooked all the way through. Are you thinking this could be a new addition to our cake range?"

"It's possible. Maybe we could showcase it when we have a historical weekend. This would be perfect when we have the visiting lecturers talk about the Roman archeological remains found in the grounds."

He grunted. "That's not the worst idea I've ever heard."

I took that as a compliment. Chef Heston didn't know how to give those.

"Chef, I wanted to check something with you."

"Go on." He kept his gaze on my honey bread.

"The night Kendal Jakes died, did you find a mess in the kitchen when you arrived in the morning?"

His head lifted. "Was that you?"

"No! I always clear up at the end of the day."

His mouth twisted to the side. "Hmmm. Someone raided the cheese, bread, and cut up a chocolate cake. They left the wreckage behind. Who was it?"

"Lord Rupert's friends, I think."

He scowled. "Typical."

That confirmed Simon and Christian had been here and not killing Kendal in the woods.

To my surprise, Chef Heston patted me on the shoulder. "Interesting work, Holly. Keep it up."

I stared at him as he strode away. What had gotten into him? He was usually so critical of everything I did.

I was getting used to his surly ways. He behaved that way because he had such high standards for his kitchen and expected his staff to give their very best every day.

As much as I got riled by his shouting, he did it for the right reasons.

I lifted the honey bread and inspected it. My gaze went to the window just as Rupert strode past.

Setting the bread quickly on a plate, I grabbed a knife. I had no time to sample it, but this was the perfect opportunity to present it to Rupert and see if I could put a smile back on his face.

I raced out the back door and hurried after him. "Rupert! Have you got a moment?"

He turned and nodded. "Always for you, Holly." His gaze landed on the plate. "Oooh! Is that for me?"

I bit my bottom lip. "I thought you might enjoy it. It's something I've been working on. And, well, I figured you needed cheering up after everything that's happened with Kendal."

"Oh, yes." He rubbed the back of his neck. "I'm still so surprised by it all. I keep expecting to wake up and discover it was all a bad dream. He really is dead."

"And you're not sad about that?"

His eyebrows shot up. "Well, I'm not happy. But, and I feel terrible for saying this, I don't miss him. I thought it would feel harder, losing a friend. It's not the first time I've lost a buddy. I still think about him even after all these years."

"Who did you lose?"

"Oh, it was a terrible accident one summer holiday. I was out with a group of friends and we were swimming in a lake. We shouldn't have been there, but you know what it's like, teenage boys think they're immortal. Anyway, Seb went into the water and never came out. That was over a decade ago, and I often wonder what he'd have been like if he'd lived. Please don't think me a terrible person, but I almost feel relieved that Kendal's gone. He could be a chaos maker."

I briefly touched his arm. "Alice did mention that he gave you a hard time when you were growing up. Maybe that's why you don't feel so sad."

He waved a hand in the air, his gaze not meeting mine. "He did like to joke. Maybe it'll come to me in time. Grief hits people in different ways, doesn't it?"

"You're right, it does. And these are unusual circumstances. Maybe you're still in shock."

Rupert tilted his head from side to side. "It could be that." He clapped his hands together. "Anyway, enough sad talk. How about we try this delicious looking cake? Tell me all about it."

I nodded as we walked to a bench and sat. "It's an ancient recipe."

"Brilliant! Combining your love of history and food."

I smiled. Rupert always paid attention when I talked. He knew that I'd studied history and had an interest in looking up all things Tudor related. "That's right, and this isn't a cake, but a bread. It's a recipe that originated in Roman times. Bread laced with honey."

"How interesting. A bit like a tea bread?"

"Not that sweet. I've yet to perfect the recipe, so you need to be honest with what you think. And you get to try the first slice."

"I can't wait. Let us eat cake." He chuckled. "Well, let us eat Holly's delicious honey bread."

I cut us both off a piece and handed him the first one. "Tell me exactly what you think. Is it too sweet? Not sweet enough? There are half a dozen spices in there, so it's not going to taste like your average slice of bread."

"I'm sure it will be perfection." Rupert took a big bite and chewed. He blinked rapidly. "Well, this is very ... different."

"Different good?"

He coughed as he swallowed the bread. "Um, it's very salty. Is it supposed to be?"

I took a small bite. The second I chewed I almost gagged. "Bleurgh! This is terrible. The recipe only called for a pinch of salt and a half measure of honey. Don't tell me I got them round the wrong way? I've never done that before."

Rupert went to take another bite, but I knocked the bread from his hand.

"What did you do that for?" he asked.

"You can't seriously want to eat that? All that salt won't be good for you. I'm such an idiot getting the most basic ingredients mixed up."

"Nonsense. Holly, you made it and I want to eat it."

"Please don't do it for my benefit. I'll have to try again." I rested my head in my hands for a second. I'd been distracted when I was baking. Even though I'd tried to dismiss Kendal's murder from my mind, it still lingered. "Imagine if I'd done this to something we served the customers? Chef Heston would have me scrubbing the kitchen floor for a month as punishment."

Rupert patted my hand. "It's really not that bad. Cut me another slice."

"No! This is going straight in the trash. What a waste."

"Don't give up. You'll get there in the end. You'll soon have perfected Roman honey bread, and we'll sell it to visitors in their droves. You never know, you might start a new food trend and all the food bloggers will interview you."

"They won't want to interview me if they get a taste of this monstrosity."

"Better luck next time." He scrubbed his chin before looking around. "There was something I wanted to ask you."

"Not to make any more terrible honey breads?"

He chuckled, then cleared his throat. "It's only a small thing. Do you enjoy music? It's just that there's a recital at —"

"Rupert! Get over here." Christian emerged from the garden and waved at him. "Stop chatting up your girlfriend. We've got the quad bikes out."

Rupert's cheeks flushed bright red, and he shook his head. "Ignore him. He's so uncouth."

I picked up a piece of the gross honey bread and inspected it as nerves fluttered in my stomach. "He's only teasing you."

"He should know better." Rupert pushed to his feet. "I need to get along. Enjoy your day." He strode away, encouraged by the catcalls of his friend.

My pulse sped up. It had sounded as if Rupert was about to ask me out, but that could never happen.

I looked at my failed Roman honey bread and sighed. I had to put this murder out of my mind once and for all. It was all sorted. I couldn't afford to make any more mistakes in the kitchen.

It was time to move on from my obsession with this murder and my maybe tiny crush on Rupert.

Chapter 17

The previous day had been a blur of baking, avoiding being yelled at by Chef Heston, and puzzling out the missing ingredient in my Roman honey bread.

I removed my apron and headed outside into the warm early afternoon sunshine. "Come on, Meatball. It's time for a walk."

He emerged from his luxurious kennel and stretched before bouncing over to me. I petted his head, and we headed around the side of the castle.

I let him off his leash, and he trotted along ahead of me as I stopped to admire the new memorial garden. I paused by a sign that had been installed.

A public memorial event will be held here on Thursday, June 26 at 2pm. Everyone is welcome if they wish to spend a few moments remembering a lost loved one. Details of plaques available for purchase will also be on hand. There will be somebody to speak to you about how you can make the best use of the memorial garden.

That was such a lovely thing to do. It was a perfect way to remember somebody, especially if you didn't have an opportunity to visit their grave.

I was surprised to see several plaques with names and dates already in place in the memorial garden.

As I explored them, I noticed the name Sebastien Grenville. He'd only been seventeen years old when he'd died. That was no age. If he'd been alive, he'd be the same age as Rupert and his friends.

Sebastien? When I'd spoken to Rupert yesterday, he'd mentioned the death of his friend, Seb. Could this be the same person? Perhaps Rupert had placed the plaque here. If he had, it was just another example of how thoughtful he was.

I had to stop thinking like that. I wasn't falling for the lord of the manor.

After walking Meatball for half an hour, I tucked him back in his kennel. I had ten minutes until I needed to be back at work, and that gave me just enough time to run to the private family library.

The Duchess had said I could access it, and I wanted to take a look at Rupert's old school yearbooks. Maybe there was a record of his friend Sebastien.

I inhaled deeply as I entered the warm, sun-dappled library. Floor-to-ceiling bookcases lined the walls, and they were crammed full of alluring books. I often enjoyed wiling away a few hours with a historical adventure or a mouth wateringly good cook book.

The expensive and rare books were kept hidden behind glass and away from everyday access, but I quickly found rows of school yearbooks going back decades.

I pulled out a yearbook during the time period Rupert would have been at school and flicked through the pages until I came to the pictures.

I ran a finger down the page. There it was. Sebastien Grenville. That must have been who Rupert was talking about. The friend who drowned in the lake.

The picture was slightly faded, but showed a serious young man, with curly dark hair and an intense expression in his dark eyes, as if he was trying to stare through the camera lens and into the soul of the photographer.

I placed the yearbook down and took out my phone. I typed in Sebastien's full name and paired it with lake accident. Several archived newspapers came online.

He'd died in a swimming accident when out with his friends. They'd accessed a lake that had been out of bounds because the water was very deep and cold.

"What are you up to?"

I jumped and spun around. Tony Bambridge stood in the doorway of the library.

"Oh! You just caught me being nosy." I pushed my phone back in my pocket.

He strolled in and looked around the library. "Places like this always remind me of my old school days. All the hours of enforced learning and exams. I've never found a use for quadrangles and equations."

"Same here. Although I did appreciate learning how to convert all the different measurements for baking. Otherwise you get in a muddle when it comes to imperial, metric, and measuring spoons."

He shrugged and his gaze went to the table where I'd placed the book. "Hey! Is that an old Eton yearbook?"

I rested a hand on top of it. "Yes. Lord Rupert mentioned a friend who died when you were younger. I was curious about him."

He lifted his chin. "Oh, that's right. Sebastien. I haven't thought about him for ages."

"Do you mind me asking what happened?"

"I guess not. It was just one of those sad things. We were fooling around like idiots, and Kendal dared Seb to swim to the middle of the lake and dive as far as he could.

It was such a Kendal thing to do, and Seb was always trying to impress him, so he went along with it."

"Was Kendal the leader of your group?"

He shrugged again. "He probably liked to think he was. We warned Seb not to do it. He wasn't a great swimmer, but he got riled up. He said he could easily swim that far. So we let him. In fact, we stood at the edge of the lake and cheered him on. Kendal was the worst. He kept yelling that he was a coward, and he'd never do it. The last time I saw Seb alive was when he shot us a rude hand gesture and then dived beneath the water. At first, we all cheered him on. Then he didn't surface. Thirty seconds and we were still cheering. Then it became a minute. That's when we panicked."

"What happened to him?"

"The paramedics reckon he got caught in weeds on the bottom of the lake bed or got a cramp. He could even have swallowed water and become confused and been swimming the wrong way. Nobody knows for sure."

"Did you try to get him out?"

Tony shot me an irritated look. "Of course. We dived in while Rupert called for an ambulance. At first, I thought Seb was joking. I imagined he'd resurfaced on the other side of the lake and was laughing his head off at us idiots trying to rescue him. But he never came up. We didn't find him. It was only after the paramedics turned up and called in the police dive team that they discovered him. By then, there was nothing anyone could do. He'd been underwater for a good hour." He shook his head and looked away.

"That's tragic."

Tony nodded. "It's almost as if this group is cursed."

"What makes you say that?"

"Two of us dead. We've even joked about that ourselves. Two eligible young bachelors dead before the world saw everything they had to offer."

My heart lurched. Could these two deaths be connected? Maybe it was nothing, but now I'd caught hold of the idea, I couldn't let it go. Sebastian dead from a tragic accident, an accident Kendal was involved in, and now Kendal had been murdered. Had his past come back to haunt him?

"Were you close to Kendal?" I asked.

"Not particularly. We ran into a spot of bother when it came to a business deal six months ago. Things between us soured after that."

"I heard that you lent him money, and the investment didn't work out."

He arched an eyebrow. "Did you now. It happens. It was my own fault for losing that investment."

"You weren't angry with Kendal that the business never took off?"

"Sure I was." He jiggled on the balls of his feet. "I let our friendship blind me. Kendal was often coming up with ridiculous business ideas and then never seeing them through. I was impressed when he came to me with some initial financing in place and a business plan. That's where I slipped up. I didn't look at it properly. If I had, I'd have seen it was simply a copy and paste job. He'd taken a load of ideas and outlines from other plans and put his name to them. It was a rookie move, and I fell for it because we were friends. I wanted to give him a break."

"How much did you lose?"

"Half a million."

"That's a lot of money." And it gave him the perfect motive for murder.

Tony's eyes narrowed, and he took a step closer. "Why are you asking all these questions about Kendal? You didn't know him. He's nothing to you."

"That's true, but he did die in the place I live."

Tony sneered. "Don't go getting ideas above your station. You work in the kitchens at the castle. You're hardly going to be the next duchess. Have I got a little snoop on my hands? What did you think you were going to do, figure this murder out so you could get in Rupert's good books? Don't think I haven't noticed the way he looks at you."

My eyes widened. "I don't know what you mean. He doesn't look at me in any way."

He smirked. "He was always a sucker for a sad story."

"My story's not sad. I have a really great life."

"What did you tell Rupert to get him to go all goo-goo eyes over you? That you're an orphan and nobody loves you?"

"I have plenty of people who care about me. I'm not deceiving Lord Rupert about anything. I'm simply curious about what happened to one of his friends. It seems that there are a number of people who wanted Kendal dead."

"Are you including me in that?"

I licked my lips. "He did lose you a lot of money. I'd have been angry if a friend cheated me out of all that cash."

He lifted a hand before dropping it. "Don't go pointing the finger at me. I didn't kill him. I've got plenty of money. Giving some to Kendal was simply a waste. I've learned my lesson. And it looks like Kendal's learned his lesson as well. He can't cheat anyone else now."

Here was another person who clearly had no fond feelings for his dead friend. "Remind me again where you were when Kendal died?"

Tony took another step closer. "No. That's none of your business. Why don't you scuttle back to the kitchen like a good girl?"

I looked around as worry flickered through me. We were alone.

"Don't go spreading some nasty little rumor that I had anything to do with Kendal's murder. We all know it was

Izzie. She's behind this. You don't need to cause trouble for me."

"I'm not causing trouble. I'm trying to get to the truth."

"Everyone knows what the truth is. Leave this alone."

I backed away and bumped into a chair.

The library door opened. The Duke strolled in, holding several books. "Oh! There are people in my library."

"My apologies, Your Grace." I turned and hurried to the door, grateful for the distraction. "The Duchess said I may use the library to do research on my recipes."

He squinted at me as if he'd never seen me before in his life. "Very good. I always enjoy a feast from the kitchen." His gaze drifted to Tony. "Are you here to repair the chandelier?"

"Oh, no. I'm a friend of Rupert's. We've met before." Tony strode over and held his hand out to the Duke.

The Duke simply peered at him before nodding. "One of his school friends, no doubt." He wandered off to the bookshelves.

Tony glared at me one more time before striding out of the library.

I waited for a few seconds before hurrying out myself.

Tony's behavior was suspicious. And even I might be tempted to kill someone if they lost me all that money. No matter what he said, it must have stung to lose so much and be deceived by a friend.

Why did he want to keep me quiet? If there was no reason to doubt his innocence, then he should have no objections to me asking questions.

I knew it. I should have listened to my gut instinct. This mystery wasn't over yet.

Chapter 18

"Phew! What a day." Louise grinned at me as she pulled off her apron. "I'm going home and putting my foot spa on for the evening. My feet feel like they've swollen to twice the size, I've been on them so long today."

"Mine too," I said. "The sunshine brought out so many visitors today."

"You're not going anywhere." Chef Heston strode in with an empty cake stand in his hand. "Lord Rupert has requested afternoon tea. And he wants you to take it to him."

I glanced at the clock. "It's six o'clock. Shouldn't he have dinner now?"

"You're questioning Lord Rupert's request?"

"Absolutely not! He can have afternoon tea for breakfast if he wants."

"Choose a selection from the fresh pastries in the chiller. And hurry up about it," Chef Heston said.

I nodded. I'd hoped to get finished on time this evening so I'd have a chance to think about my talk with Tony and what my next move should be. That wasn't going to happen now.

I said goodbye to Louise, then hurried around the kitchen and prepared the afternoon tea. I selected fresh scones with a pot of clotted cream and strawberry preserves, mini chocolate eclairs, dark chocolate brownies, and a selection of crustless sandwiches. I brewed tea in Rupert's favorite china teapot and placed everything on a trolley. I wheeled it through the castle toward Rupert's private quarters.

I slowed as raised voices came from the great drawing room. The door was slightly open, and I crept over and peered through the gap.

It was Chris and Simon. Chris stood with his hands clenched, and Simon's face was bright red and his hair stood on end as if he'd been running his hands through it.

"You need to keep quiet." Chris glared at Simon. "There's nothing to worry about. This will blow over soon."

Simon paced around the room. "I'm not so sure. I don't think she was involved."

"Of course she was. Izzie was obsessed with Kendal. She's been like that since we were teenagers, chasing after him like some lost puppy. It was humiliating. I even pulled Izzie aside and told her she needed a new hobby. She wouldn't listen to me. She was determined to have Kendal to herself."

I bit my bottom lip. They were discussing Kendal's murder.

Simon shook his head. "Izzie's different now. She's changed."

"She hasn't changed. Otherwise, why was she hanging around outside the castle the night Kendal was killed? She was hoping to get a glimpse of him. That's pathetic."

Simon strode toward Chris. "I've already told you, it can't be her. She was with me the night of his murder."

My eyes widened, and I clapped a hand over my mouth. Izzie was innocent!

"Listen, mate, she may have been with you for some of that evening, but she was still into Kendal. I haven't told you this until now, because I know you like her, but when I picked Kendal up for this weekend, Izzie was at his apartment."

"Huh? What was she doing there?"

"Looking unhappy. I didn't expect to find her there, but Kendal said she'd turned up unexpectedly, demanding to see him. He let her in because he didn't want the neighbors complaining about her shouting in the street and causing another scene."

Simon dropped into a seat and rubbed his forehead. "Izzie said she liked me. She never mentioned that she was still seeing Kendal."

"Which goes to show you can't trust her." Chris settled in the seat next to Simon and thumped him on the back. "There are far better girls out there for you. More stable ones. Ones less likely to jerk you around, and you can take them home to the family without causing a scandal."

Simon's shoulders slumped. "But ... I like her."

"She's bad for you, mate. She was cheating on you with Kendal."

"Maybe you've gotten things wrong. Did Kendal actually say they were still together?"

"She wanted to be with him. For all you know, Izzie could have been seeing you to get closer to Kendal. Or maybe she thought she'd make him jealous if he figured out you were dating. Whatever was going on in her head, it wasn't normal. She's guilty."

"She can't be guilty of Kendal's murder. She was with me."

"You want to keep quiet about that," Chris said. "For all we know, the police don't have the timings right for when

Kendal died. They can never be a hundred percent sure of the exact time of death. It's all guesswork."

"It's a bit more than guesswork."

"Sure, but it's a couple of hours either way. Izzie could have slipped out in the night and met up with Kendal. She might even have been to see him after she'd spent time with you."

"I can't believe that," Simon said. "She was with me when he died."

"If you change your story now, it will look suspicious. It'll also look bad for me. You're my alibi. We're covering for each other."

Simon was silent for a moment. "You ... didn't do it, did you? I mean, I know you had a few problems with Kendal."

"Of course not! I don't want to go to prison. Kendal's not worth that sacrifice. Mate, we're best buddies. Don't forget the code of honor we've had since school. Friends first. Our friendship will last forever. Girls come and go. They always will. We're in this for life."

Simon chuckled darkly. "It's almost as if we're married."

"That's the spirit." Chris slapped him on the back again. "There's no chance of getting a divorce from me. It's the friendships that are important. We look out for each other. None of us killed Kendal. Sure, he could be a massive pain in the behind. He messed with us all with his dumb jokes. None of that mattered. He was a part of the group. We don't stab each other in the back."

"What about Izzie?" Simon asked. "I can't let her go to prison for something she didn't do."

"You have to move on from this girl. She's bad for you. Don't do anything stupidly heroic and claim you killed Kendal," Chris said. "That won't solve anything."

"I wasn't planning on doing that. But I could give the police an anonymous tipoff."

"Which would drag you straight back into this whole mess. Izzie cheated on you. If she's not guilty of murder, then she's guilty of that. Good riddance to her. You don't want someone like that in your life. She'd drag you down if you associate with her and her bad reputation."

Simon sighed. "Maybe you're right. I mean, she should have told me the truth about being involved with Kendal."

Shock filtered through me. He couldn't go along with this. Simon knew that Izzie was innocent. And since Simon had been with Izzie when Kendal was killed, that made them both innocent, but what about Christian? Was he the killer?

I'd picked up nothing suspicious about him when we'd spoken. He'd seemed like a decent guy. Had he deceived me? Had he deceived everyone and was trying to pin the murder he'd committed on Izzie?

"Who are we listening to?"

I jumped and spun around. "Lady Philippa!" It was the first time I'd seen her out of her rooms. "What are you ... I mean, how are you here?"

She chuckled. "I tested your theory. The door to my prison was unlocked. It must have been an error on the part of my jailer. I saw an opportunity to escape and took it. So, come on, who are you eavesdropping on?"

I pressed a finger to my lips and then realized how disrespectful that was and blushed. She was, after all, a proper lady with a capital L. It wasn't my place to shush her.

She waved a hand in the air, dismissing my impropriety. "Tell me everything. This has to do with the murder, doesn't it?"

Before I had a chance to speak, the door to the great drawing room was pulled open. Christian stood there, glaring at us. "Lady Philippa. It's a pleasure to see you again." He caught hold of her hand and went to kiss the back of it, but she pulled it away.

"There's no need for that. What are you two doing in there?" She peered past Christian.

Simon hurried to the door and joined him. "Lady Philippa, always a pleasure."

"I'm sure it is. You still haven't answered my question. We're very interested in your conversation. Discussing murder, are you?"

I shot her a startled look. Lady Philippa might be immune to the attentions of Christian and Simon, but I wasn't. I didn't have the back up of an elite private security team looking out for me if things went the wrong way.

Christian wrapped an arm tightly around Simon's shoulders and hustled him out of the door. "Murder! Nothing like that. We were talking about... sport."

"And women," Simon stammered.

Lady Philippa arched an eyebrow. "You need to refine your topics of conversation, or you'll never keep a lady interested. We need stimulating conversation."

"Absolutely. We'll get to work on that right away. Come on, Simon." Christian dragged him away.

"Girl, we need to talk." Lady Philippa grabbed my arm with surprisingly strong fingers for such a tiny woman, and we headed back to her rooms.

She let out a sigh of relief as she settled in her chair. "That's quite enough escaping for one day. So, tell me everything you heard those two boys say. I know they weren't talking about sport and ladies."

I was still trying to pull my thoughts in order after everything I'd just heard. "There's a problem."

"With the murder investigation," she said. "So my prediction tells me."

I nodded, still not certain about her prediction's accuracy. "What did it reveal to you?"

"That no one is safe. A killer is still on the loose, despite the police arresting someone."

"I think you're right."

"No thinking needed. I know I'm right. That young girl they've arrested is innocent."

"And I know who really killed Kendal," I said. "During their conversation, Simon admitted that Izzie was with him at the time Kendal was killed. Christian was doing his best to convince him to keep quiet. Simon is his alibi. If he reveals the truth to the police, Christian has no one backing him up."

"And he could easily have taken Kendal outside for a cigar and a brandy and whacked him on the back of the head. He wouldn't have thought twice about going for a late night stroll with an old friend."

"The police have the wrong person. Izzie didn't do it."

Lady Philippa clutched her chest and gasped.

"What's wrong? Is it your heart?" I raced over and kneeled beside her.

"Just a … prediction." She grabbed my hand. "Oh! Holly, you must be careful. I see dark times ahead of you. They're charging toward you as we speak. Danger is approaching."

"Danger! Coming for me? You don't think Christian's going to try to keep me quiet? I have to report what I've heard to the police, or at least tell Campbell. That will stop him."

She shook her head. "Campbell is part of your problem. He's the danger I'm seeing."

"Campbell?" That had to be a mistake. "Lady Philippa, perhaps you've overexerted yourself. All that excitement of leaving your room. You should rest. Campbell protects everyone in the castle. He'd never hurt me."

She was quiet for a moment, her hand trembling as she still clung to me. "I am feeling tired. But don't forget my words. You're in real trouble."

"What should I do to get out of trouble?" I helped her out of her chair and over to her bedroom.

"I'd suggest making a run for it, but that would only make you look guilty."

"Guilty of what?"

"All I see is darkness and fear in your future." She settled back on her silk pillows and closed her eyes.

Horatio opened one eye before shuffling over and resting his head on her stomach.

"So, what should I do?" Her words sounded so sincere that I found myself believing them. But Lady Philippa couldn't be right about this. Why was I in danger from Campbell?

She closed her eyes but didn't speak.

I wanted to nudge her, ask her how I was supposed to get away from this danger, but I didn't like to push. However these predictions happened, they exhausted her.

After a few moments, Lady Philippa appeared to be asleep, her chest rising and falling at regular intervals. I tucked a cashmere blanket around her and then walked slowly out of her rooms and back down the stone stairs.

If Christian had killed Kendal, he wouldn't make a move on me. If he did, Lady Philippa would be able to tell everyone what had happened.

I grimaced. It had better not get that far.

I hurried back to my abandoned trolley of cakes and tea. I checked the teapot and frowned. The tea was lukewarm and looked stewed. I'd have to go back to the kitchen and get a fresh pot. If I got caught doing that by Chef Heston then I'd know all about real trouble. Maybe this was the darkness Lady Philippa had seen. Chef Heston shouting at me. If that was the worst that was going to happen to me tonight, I could handle it.

I reversed the trolley and turned it around in the hall. I froze to the spot as Campbell loomed in front of me.

I blew out a breath and tried to slow my racing heart. "I wish you wouldn't do that."

"Do what?" he asked.

"Your creepy silent spy behavior moves. My nerves are already frayed this evening."

"Then prepare for them to be even more frayed. Holly Holmes, you're under arrest for the murder of Kendal Jakes."

Chapter 19

I stared at Campbell, my fingers gripping the trolley as Lady Philippa's words flooded back to me. "Is this payback because I've been asking questions that I shouldn't?"

"No joke. I'm deadly serious."

My eyes narrowed. He did look super serious and a bit intimidating. "I have a delivery to make. Can you arrest me later?"

He didn't even blink. "No."

Oh my goodness, this was really happening. "Why do you think I'm involved in Kendal's murder?"

"I'm taking you to the police station for formal questioning. You'll learn everything then. Unless you'd like to confess now."

I backed away, my heart pounding. "I didn't do it."

"Don't make this difficult, Holly."

My hands grew clammy as my heart beat out an unhealthily fast rhythm.

"And don't even think about running." Campbell strode over and grabbed my arm.

"I wasn't going to." The panic-filled portion of my brain absolutely was thinking that, but I'd only make it five steps before Campbell tackled me to the ground.

I allowed him to escort me out of the castle to the waiting black car.

Campbell settled in the driver's seat. Saracen was next to him. I was in the back, feeling guilty as heck, even though I had nothing to worry about.

"What makes you think I killed Kendal?" I asked as the car pulled away.

Neither of them replied.

"You need to give me a hint. Should I call a lawyer?"

"That's your privilege," Campbell said. "Do you think you need one?"

"I'm innocent, but it sounds like you don't think so. Why is that?"

I got no reply to that question.

I took a few deep, steadying breaths as I tried to make sense of this. I should have stayed out of this just like Campbell told me to. If I hadn't poked around and gotten involved, I'd have my feet up on the couch, snuggling with Meatball and thinking about what to have for dinner. My Granny Molly always said I was too nosy for my own good. That was definitely the case this time around.

The drive to the police station only took ten minutes. Once we were parked, Saracen climbed out and waited outside.

Campbell turned to me in his seat. "Just answer the questions. Don't conceal anything."

"Are you sure this isn't a joke?" It was the only explanation I could drag up to make sense of this.

"As I'm sure you're already aware, I don't do jokes."

"Which means you've got something on me. What is it? Please, just a hint."

"Let's move." He climbed out of the car and opened the door for me.

For a second, I considered protesting and not moving, but Campbell would only pull me out and drag me into the station.

There was nothing I could do but follow him into the station with Saracen guarding my back in case I made a run for it, and await my fate.

"Is the interview room ready?" Campbell asked the female police officer standing at the reception desk.

"All ready for use, sir."

I felt dizzy as I was escorted past the reception desk and along a beige corridor into a small room with only a table and chairs in it.

"Is this room soundproofed?" I asked as I settled in my seat.

"Doubtful. Why do you want to know?" Campbell asked.

"If it is, you can torture anything you like out of me and no one will know."

He sighed as he sat in the seat opposite me. "Holly, this is deadly serious."

"I get that now. I still don't know why you think I'm involved with murdering Kendal, though. You'd discounted me as a suspect."

The door opened, and a police officer walked in. He nodded at Campbell and glanced at me before sitting in the only spare seat.

"This is Detective Inspector Gerald from the Cambridgeshire constabulary," Campbell said. "He's been supporting the investigation at the castle."

I recognized him from my many trips into Audley St. Mary doing my cake deliveries. He had a long thin face and a broad nose. He looked like he was in need of a good night's sleep. He placed a notepad on the desk alongside a pen and a file.

Campbell nodded at him before his attention returned to me. "Let's start with your relationship with Kendal Jakes."

"I had no relationship with him," I said. "I didn't know him."

"You met him when he came to stay at the castle, is that correct?"

"Only once." I glanced from Campbell to the police inspector. "And only for a few minutes. I delivered some desserts to Lord Rupert and his friends the first night they arrived."

"What impression did you have of Kendal after meeting him?" Campbell asked.

"He'd been drinking and was perhaps a little over friendly."

"He made an inappropriate advance toward you?"

"Kendal was just a bit crass. But I've already told you this. It isn't new information."

"And now you're telling me again," Campbell said. "You must have been annoyed by his behavior."

"I've had much worse. And Lord Rupert stepped in, as did his other friends. It was over in a moment. I left and forgot all about it."

"Yet you continued to poke around in the murder investigation. Why is that?" Campbell asked.

"Because I don't believe Izzie's guilty."

Campbell's eyes narrowed. "Is that because you killed Kendal and you're feeling bad about it?"

"No!" I tapped on the top of the table. "I've found out that Izzie's innocent. I overheard a conversation between Simon and Christian. Izzie was with Simon when Kendal was killed. She couldn't have done it."

Campbell glanced at Detective Inspector Gerald. "Did you see them together?"

"No. They were most likely in Simon's bedroom. I'd have been fast asleep at the time."

"Which is where you claim to be when Kendal was murdered." Detective Inspector Gerald consulted the file he'd brought in.

"I don't claim anything. That's exactly where I was."

"Yet you only had your dog as an alibi."

"You're not listening to me. Christian insisted that Simon covered for him. Simon is lying to protect his friend. You shouldn't have me in here; you need to speak to Christian."

"Why are you trying so hard to shift attention from yourself? Do you have something to hide?" Detective Inspector Gerald asked.

"I'm hiding nothing. And I'm not deflecting attention. I'm trying to help."

"You began by tailing Miss Northcott and spreading rumors that she killed Kendal. When that failed, you targeted someone else. Explain your actions."

"They're the actions of a woman determined to get to the truth. A concept you appear to have great difficulty coming to terms with."

Campbell cleared his throat. "Let's keep this civil, Holly."

"You'll have to excuse me if I'm spiky, but you're trying to pin this murder on me. I'm not letting that happen. Tell me why I'm here."

Campbell and Detective Inspector Gerald exchanged a glance.

Campbell nodded. "Very well. We have evidence that you murdered Kendal."

This was the information I'd been waiting to hear. "What's the evidence?"

"Your fingerprints are on the murder weapon."

The air felt like it vanished from the room. I tried to breathe, but all I heard was a strange wheezing gasp coming from my mouth.

I clutched the edge of the table and stared at Campbell. "What was the murder weapon?"

Detective Inspector Gerald leaned forward. "Why don't you tell us what you used? I'll put in a good word and say you cooperated. That could go in your favor when it comes to sentencing."

My mind blanked as my hands shook. I had to get control of this situation. "Tell me my motive, present me with witnesses, and provide a timeline of my movements leading up to Kendal's murder."

"We're working on that," Detective Inspector Gerald said.

"You'll be working for a long time, because I didn't do it." I checked in with Campbell. A glitter of something I couldn't determine appeared in his gaze.

"The murder weapon was a spade," he said.

"Then there's no way it was me. If you'd said a heavy frying pan or a cast iron griddle, I can get my hands on plenty of those, but I haven't been anywhere near any garden tools. I can't even remember the last time ..." My eyes widened, and I swallowed.

"What is it?" Campbell's brow lowered. "What have you remembered?"

"I mean, it's possible my fingerprints were found on a spade, but not because I used it to kill Kendal. A few days ago, I helped the gardeners load up their tools when they'd finished with the new memorial garden. I picked up all sorts of equipment. Was that where the spade was found?"

"Why don't you tell us where you left it?" Detective Inspector Gerald said.

I barely resisted the urge to be rude. My freedom was at stake. "Nowhere, because I didn't kill Kendal."

"Your fingerprints were the freshest on the spade. You'd done a poor job wiping off the prints. Plus, there were traces of Kendal's blood on the weapon," Detective Inspector Gerald said.

"Where did I hide this evidence laden murder weapon?" My voice wobbled.

"It was found among the tools used by the gardeners," Campbell said.

"That was clever, hiding it there. I expect you hoped it would get used, and the evidence destroyed," Detective Inspector Gerald said.

My head whipped from side to side. "I didn't kill Kendal! Why would I do that?"

Campbell leaned back in his seat. What looked like disappointment flickered across his face. He'd given up on me.

"If you confess now, we might do a deal. From your account given to Campbell, it's plausible that Kendal pressed unwanted advances on you. If Lord Rupert and his friends support that, the sentence may be reduced," Detective Inspector Gerald said.

"Sentence! Nope, no way. This is wrong. I didn't kill him. I didn't appreciate him making crass comments, but I wouldn't kill someone because of that. Campbell, you have to believe me. You know me."

He glanced away. "I thought I did. I'm usually an excellent judge of character. You have a bad alibi for the night. No one can corroborate where you were. Trust me, I've asked around."

"Plus, your fingerprints are on the murder weapon. I suspect a search of your apartment will reveal mud on your clothing and shoes from the site the body was buried," Detective Inspector Gerald said, a hint of smugness in his tone. He thought he'd solved this case.

"You most likely will find exactly that," I said. "You seem to have forgotten that I discovered the body with

Princess Alice. I stomped around in the mud for ages. And I often go to that site to walk my dog."

"And that's another thing." Detective Inspector Gerald had a triumphant gleam in his eyes. "You knew where the body was."

"No!" Jeez, how did this guy ever get to be an inspector? "You've got this all turned around. My dog, Meatball, smelled the body and took us to it. I had no clue Kendal was buried in the woods. And it makes no sense to take Meatball into the woods if I'd buried a body there. I know what he's like, he can sniff out a disgusting smell from miles away. I'm telling you the truth. This has nothing to do with me."

The door to the interview room burst open. Lord Rupert stumbled in, a large bandage stuck to his right forehead. His eyes widened as he saw me. Right behind him was a tall, imposing man in an expensive suit, holding a briefcase.

"I demand you let Holly Holmes go immediately," Rupert said, bright dots of color bursting on each cheek.

Campbell stood. "Lord Rupert, we're simply questioning Holly. There are no formal charges being brought at this stage."

"Which means she's free to go." Rupert gestured for me to stand. "If you have anything more to say to her, you do it through the family lawyer. Smitherington will deal with any inquiries. And the next time you drag a member of my staff in for questioning, you will inform me first. She's an invaluable member of the team, and to have her dragged away from her duties with no warning is unacceptable."

Campbell pulled back his shoulders and clasped his hands in front of him. "It's for your own safety, sir. The safety of the family overrides any other inconveniences."

Rupert pulled himself up to his not insubstantial height and glared at Campbell. "Do not forget who your employer is."

"I would never do that, sir. But—"

"Holly, you're with me." Rupert held out his hand.

I thought about taking hold of it, but then jumped from my seat and hurried past him. I glanced back to see Campbell and Detective Inspector Gerald glaring at me.

I wasn't out of trouble just yet, but it looked like I'd been given a short reprieve.

Rupert muttered under his breath as he strode alongside me, the lawyer right behind us.

"What happened to your head?" I whispered.

"Oh! An accident. One of the buggies used by the grounds people went out of control. I almost got run over." He touched the bandage. "I whacked my head on a stone pot when I fell."

I tried to feel sympathetic, but I wouldn't have been surprised if he'd been reading a book and not noticed the buggy heading his way.

There was a car waiting for us outside. Rupert ushered me into the back, alongside his lawyer.

He let out a breath as the car pulled away before reaching over and grabbing my hand. "Holly, I'm so sorry about this. The second I heard what happened, I was on the phone to Smitherington. I don't know what Campbell's playing at."

I gently eased my hand away. "I do. They have the murder weapon. It's got my fingerprints on it."

He blinked rapidly. "Well, I mean, that doesn't mean you did it."

"It absolutely doesn't," I said. "I'm as surprised as you. I can only assume the spade used to kill Kendal was hidden amongst the gardeners' tools."

"Go back to the beginning, Miss Holmes. Lay out the facts for me," Smitherington said. "Lord Rupert was a trifle panicked when he contacted me. The murder weapon was a spade?"

I nodded. "I don't know exactly where it was found, but it was among the gardeners' tools and had a set of my fingerprints on it."

"Maybe whoever used it thought the evidence would be wiped away if they placed it with this other gardening equipment," Rupert said. "That's not enough evidence to charge Holly with murder, is it?" He addressed the question to Smitherington.

"Not for definite, but I need more context," Smitherington said.

"Campbell said the police found other smudged fingerprints on the spade, but mine were the most recent," I said. "There were also traces of Kendal's blood."

"I shall need to see this evidence," Smitherington said. "Before I do, I have a question for you, Miss Holmes. How do the police have your fingerprints on record?"

"Oh, that." I gripped the underside of my seat. "My, um, well, it's nothing. My granny used to take me on protest marches when I was younger. We got caught up in a protest that turned nasty in London when I was eighteen. The police arrested us. We were fingerprinted but not charged with anything."

"I never had you down as such a rebel." Rupert smiled at me. "That's it? No other crimes in your past?"

I nodded. "I'd forgotten about it. Granny Molly said that sort of thing happened to her so often that they must have a room dedicated just to her record." I decided not to mention the other criminal activities she took part in, the ones she was behind bars for. The less they knew about her the better.

"Your granny's a criminal?" Smitherington was good; he must have sensed I was withholding something.

"Um, well, it's complicated. Her heart's in the right place."

He nodded. "The most important thing for us to do is solidify your alibi during the timeframe the murder was committed. Once we prove it's impossible for you to have been in the location at the time of the murder, you're in the clear. As you said, you could have moved the spade quite innocently. You had no idea it was the murder weapon."

"There's a problem with that. I was on my own during the time of the murder. I don't have anyone to back me up."

"Ah! That may complicate things." Smitherington glanced at Rupert.

"Holly would never do such a thing," he said. "I'll vouch for her. If this goes to trial, I'll be her character witness."

"You'd do that for me?" My eyes filled with tears, which I blinked away quickly.

His smile was warm. "Of course. Holly, you're important to me. I mean, this household. The castle wouldn't be the same without your famous cupcakes."

I choked back my tears and nodded. "Of course."

Smitherington cleared his throat. "Your character statement will lend weight to Holly's good character, if it comes to that."

The car pulled up outside the castle.

"Holly, you come with me. Smitherington, do you need us for anything else?" Rupert asked.

"I'll take the car back to the police station and gather all the evidence. I will wish to speak to you at a later date, Holly, if we can't get rid of these charges straightaway."

"Of course. Whatever you need." I climbed out of the car with Rupert. "Thanks so much for getting me out of there. I promise you, I'll pay back however much you get charged for using your lawyer."

Rupert waved a hand in the air as the car drove away. "Nonsense. Don't even think about that. Holly, we're … good friends. I believe you're innocent. All of this is a mistake. I'll have Campbell in front of you apologizing by dawn. I should have him fired for what he's done."

"Oh, no. I mean, he's wrong to think I'm involved, but he's only doing his job. He's protecting you and the family. There is evidence against me, but I assure you, I didn't do it."

"Holly!" Alice raced out the door. She flung her arms around me before kissing my head. "What a beastly business."

Meatball raced out of the castle and bounced around me.

I scooped him into my arms, glad to have him back as I snuggled him against me. "I bet you're wondering what's going on. You've missed dinner and your walk."

"I fed him and walked him," Alice said proudly. "As soon as we heard what was going on, I sent Rupert off to deal with things. I knew you'd be worried about Meatball, so I've been looking after him."

Meatball now sported a rather fetching pink bow on his collar. "Thanks. I really appreciate it. All of it." I set Meatball back on the ground.

"We're looking after you," she said. "This has been a shock for all of us. I can only imagine how awful you feel."

"There's really no need." But I didn't protest as Alice led me through the door and into her private parlor.

"You sit right there." She pointed to a comfortable looking pink chair. "We're going to wait on you hand and foot, just like you do us. We can't have our favorite member of staff thinking we don't trust her."

"I don't know what to say." I was too stunned to argue as I sank down.

"Rupert, bring that footstool over. Then go to the kitchen and sort out some delicious treats for Holly," Alice ordered.

"Of course." He grabbed the footstool and gently placed my feet on it. "Is there anything else I can get you?"

"Really, you're both too kind. I just want this all over with."

"Smitherington is the best lawyer you can get. He can make the guiltiest look innocent," Rupert said. "Of course, not that either of us think you're guilty. But with him on your side, you're guaranteed to have this dealt with in no time. Campbell and the police are incompetent."

"Of course they are," Alice said.

I sat back as they talked about how awful it was and all the lovely things they had planned to make it up to me.

This was such a shock, and I had no idea what to do next. The amazing life I'd been building in the castle could be over. If the police pursued this, I could lose my job, my home, and if the worst happened, I'd get charged with murder and go to prison. I wouldn't be able to take Meatball with me. I'd lose him too.

I shook my head as I pinched the bridge of my nose. How had everything gone so wrong so fast? It felt like I was about to lose everything.

Chapter 20

I'd kept a low profile yesterday after being taken in for questioning.

Rupert had told Chef Heston that I was under the weather and needed a day off. I'd appreciated having the time to myself, but I'd hidden in my room, not sure what to do.

I couldn't hide forever. These might be my last few days of freedom. I wasn't going to spend them cowering and worrying about what the police were cooking up for me.

I had to believe in Rupert's lawyer and trust the truth would come out. And, if that failed, I needed to make sure I spent my last days as a free woman doing the things I loved. And that meant going to the kitchen.

After I'd settled Meatball in his kennel, I opened the kitchen door and peeked around the side.

It was the usual busy hive of activity, with people rushing around as Chef Heston barked orders.

His gaze flickered to the door, and he strode toward me.

I pulled back, expecting him to start yelling and telling me to get out of his kitchen.

To my surprise, he caught hold of my elbow and gently guided me to the table. "How are you feeling?"

I blinked up at him. "Better, thanks. Is it okay that I'm here?"

"Of course it is. You work here."

"Oh, it's just that, well, with everything that's going on, I didn't think you ..." My voice wavered and I clamped my lips together.

He gently patted my arm. "Let me get you a mug of tea before you get started. If you feel up to working."

My eyebrows shot up. Chef Heston had never made me tea before. "That would be great. Thanks."

"Take a seat away from the chaos of my incompetent team." His glare turned lethal as he watched the rest of his team work. "I'll be right with you."

I settled on a chair, feeling almost as shocked as I'd done when Campbell took me in for questioning.

Chef Heston had a good side. All it had taken to uncover it was me getting on the hook for being a murderer.

He returned with two mugs and handed me one. "I know you weren't sick yesterday. I've heard what's going on."

My gut tightened. Was this the lead up to being fired? "It wasn't me."

He snorted before taking a sip of tea. "You don't need to tell me that. I only hire staff I trust. Within the first minute of your interview, I spotted a valuable member of staff. You were so enthusiastic about your food and poured your passion into your words. I don't make mistakes when I hire people."

I swallowed against the lump in my throat. "I'm glad you believe in me."

"I do." He jabbed a finger at me. "Most of all, I believe in your skills in the kitchen. I barely had to give you any training when you joined the team. That's a rare find. I'm not losing you to some trumped up charge. Your name will be cleared and my dessert case will return to its former cupcake laden glory. No one can make ganache icing like you can. And, if you want to keep busy, I have a job for you."

"Anything. I'm happy to get back to work. I'd actually like to keep busy. Sitting around yesterday just got my thoughts in a spin."

"Good. The food for the garden memorial event needs to be finished," he said.

"Oh! Of course. I'd forgotten all about that."

"It's happening at two o'clock this afternoon. The sandwiches are being made but all the cakes need to be iced and filled. You can add a few of your special little flourishes. Maybe mix a batch of your cream caramel frosting?"

"Absolutely." I went to stand, but Chef Heston patted me on the shoulder. "Finish your tea first. I ... I believe in you, Holly. Everything will be back to normal soon enough."

I blinked away a few tears, surprised by how much I appreciated Chef Heston's kind words.

His eyes narrowed. "Don't get all emotional on me, or I'll have to start shouting at you. No tears in my kitchen. It's forbidden."

"I'm not crying!" I swiped at my eyes. "Someone's chopping onions."

"That'll be it." A smile flashed across his face before vanishing as he walked away.

After finishing my mug of tea, I washed up in the sink, tied on an apron, and went to look at the array of cakes out on the counter ready to be finished. There were buttercream angel cakes that would look perfect with a dusting of icing sugar and sugared candy fruits decorating the top. There were several flavors of miniature sponge cake, from vanilla to chocolate. They'd look amazing with sprinkles and carefully piped cream caramel sandwiching them together. There was also a batch of chocolate cupcakes yearning to be drenched in heavenly cream swirls.

As I got to work carefully decorating the cakes, my thoughts turned to Lord Rupert. He'd most likely be at the memorial event today with his friends, remembering Sebastien.

"Holly, we need more self-raising flour and a sack of dried fruit. You'll find them in the outside store," Chef Heston said as he passed my workstation.

I finished the cake I was working on and placed my icing bag down. I also needed to get more supplies to finish off the cakes, so the distraction was welcome.

I headed to the store room located next to the kitchen and spotted Rupert walking past with a group of gardeners.

He slowed when he saw me and diverted course. "How are you doing? I didn't know you were back at work. Isn't it too soon?"

"I made the decision to come back," I said. "I needed something to keep my mind busy."

"Smitherington's still working on things. He's giving me regular updates. The police have been cooperating so far, but they're not letting this go. They've been asking around to see if they can find anyone who saw you out of your apartment during the time Kendal was murdered."

I frowned. "They're wasting their time. This is a big misunderstanding." My gaze drifted over Rupert's shoulder to the gardeners as they headed to the memorial garden. "How well do you know the team who worked on that garden?"

"Pretty well. I work alongside them several times a week. Once they got past the fact I'm a Lord, they let their guards down. They're a good bunch. Why do you ask?"

"The spade that killed Kendal was discovered among their tools," I said. "If it wasn't planted there ..." I wasn't sure where I was going with this. "Would any of them have had a grudge against Kendal?"

"Oh! No! I can't imagine any of them would," Rupert said. "Most of them are from the village. They've been helping out for years around the estate."

My mouth twisted to the side. "Not all of them are from the village? Has anyone joined in the last year that made you suspicious about them? Or perhaps asked questions about your school friends or wanted to know about their background?"

Rupert rubbed his hands together as he pondered my questions. "It's not a topic of conversation any of them have singled me out about."

"The only time I handled any gardening equipment was when I was helping pack it in the back of a car. I don't remember grabbing any spades, but I must have done. I moved some tools around so could easily have touched something without paying attention. That must be how my fingerprints got on the murder weapon."

Rupert scratched his chin. "You're wondering if the spade was planted among the gardeners' tools or if it belongs to one of them?"

I shook my head. "If it was planted, it's the perfect place. It wouldn't look odd among a jumble of other tools. And if the tools were used on a daily basis, the evidence would soon wear away when other people handled it. But … what if it's more than that?"

"It can't be anyone in that group. They're good people," Rupert said.

My gaze ran over the group as they stood by the memorial garden, giving it a final check over before the afternoon's event. Most of them were of retirement age, but there was one guy who looked to be in his late thirties, and Meredith, who was around fifty.

"Meredith has been here the same amount of time as me, hasn't she?" I said.

"Yes. She started working here three months ago, but she's been involved with the planning of the memorial garden for over a year," Rupert said. "In fact, she contacted me with the idea to set up a special place for people to remember their loved ones. She knows all about the grounds in Audley Castle because I went to school with her son."

My eyebrows shot up. I peered at Meredith. She was old enough to have had a teenage son when Rupert was at school. "Do you stay in touch with her son?"

"Sadly not. I mentioned him to you the other day. He died."

"Hang on, her son was Sebastien Grenville? Your friend who drowned?"

"Goodness, how did you know that? That's absolutely right. She'd even been here a few times with Sebastien when he was younger. When she got in touch and suggested the memorial garden, I considered it an excellent idea. It was a perfect tribute to Seb."

"And Meredith specifically wanted the garden here?"

"That's right. Hold on, you can't think she was involved with what happened to Kendal? She's a kind woman."

I bit my bottom lip as I focused on Meredith. She might be a kind person, but her son had died in an accident. What if she couldn't let it go? What if she thought Sebastien's death wasn't even an accident?

"Eton's not a cheap place to go to school. How did the son of a gardener get a space there?" I asked.

"Meredith hasn't always been a gardener. The family was well-connected. Seb's dad works in London. Something in finance." He jingled the coins in his pockets. "I'm not sure you're on the right track with this idea, though. Meredith isn't a killer."

"Whose idea was it to have the opening of the memorial garden today?" I asked.

"Oh! Well, we talked about it as a group. I wanted to make sure the memorial garden opened when my friends were here, so we could use the time to remember Seb."

"Are you sure that was your idea? Meredith didn't push for that?"

He scrubbed at his chin again. "Hmmm, now you mention it, she was keen on this date, but I didn't think anything of it."

The pieces clicked into place as my heart thudded. Meredith wasn't interested in the memorial garden. That was an excuse so she could be here at the same time as Seb's old school friends got together. She was here for revenge.

I took a step toward the gardeners and hesitated. How could I confront her? I couldn't wander over and say 'I know you killed Kendal because you blame him for your son's death'.

Rupert's hand on my arm tugged me out of my thoughts. "Whatever's the matter, Holly? You've gone very pale."

I stared up at him and licked my dry lips. What if Meredith's revenge plans were bigger? She could have seen an opportunity to kill Kendal and was waiting for more chances to get revenge on all the boys who didn't save her son.

"Oh my word! The buggy," I whispered.

"Eh? What are you talking about?" Rupert asked.

"The buggy that almost ran you over," I said. "What if Meredith used it to try to kill you?"

He stepped back. "No! It was an accident. Something went wrong with the controls."

"Has this happened before? A buggy zooming off on its own?"

"No, but it can't be anything else."

"It can. Were you on your own when the buggy came after you?"

"I was. I'd planned an evening of reading. I was looking for a spot in the grounds where I wouldn't be disturbed."

"Meredith must have been waiting, hoping to find you or one of your friends alone. She messed with the buggy controls and tried to run you over with it."

"Steady on! I ... well, I suppose it's possible. When the buggy was looked at, no one could find anything wrong with it. I simply put it down to a mechanical error. Just one of those things."

"It's very possible." I pushed against my panic. "Rupert, I need your help. You'll be at the memorial event this afternoon?"

"Of course. I can't miss it. How about you?"

I nodded. "I'll definitely be there. Meredith killed Kendal. And I think she's only just getting started."

Chapter 21

"Are you absolutely sure about this?" Alice whispered as she clutched my arm. "Do you really think Sebastien's mom will try to hurt Rupert?"

"Not for sure, but it's too much of a coincidence that Meredith came up with the plan for the memorial garden. She's engineered it so all of Sebastien's old friends are here for the opening. This is perfect for her. She gets the people she blames for her son's death in one place. That makes them easier targets."

I stood with Princess Alice, Lord Rupert, and Meatball just outside the kitchen. I'd explained everything to Rupert several times, and he was on board. We'd also decided to bring Alice in as backup.

It wouldn't look suspicious either of them being at the opening event, and I needed them to watch and see if Meredith made a move against the others in Rupert's party. I really hoped I was wrong about this, but my gut told me I wasn't.

Rupert shook his head. "I still can't believe Meredith would try to attack any of us."

"She's already had a go at you with the buggy," I said. "She might be getting desperate."

"There are too many people at the memorial event. If she tries anything, she'll be stopped. That's what our security team is for."

"Maybe she's waiting for an opportunity to get you on your own. That must be what happened with Kendal. You said he'd been drinking heavily that night. He could have slipped outside and Meredith was waiting for an opportunity to attack. She wouldn't have been able to resist taking him out when he was such an easy target."

Rupert rubbed the back of his neck. "I was surprised when she moved to Audley St. Mary once the memorial garden got underway. She used to live in London with Sebastien and his father. They've been divorced for some time. Both of them struggled to hold things together after Seb's accident."

"Which is why we know her as Meredith Jones," I said. "She must have gone back to her maiden name after the divorce."

"So, she moved to the village and planned all this?" Alice looked quizzical. "It's a big risk. How could she be certain that Rupert would host the Eton boys this year?"

I looked at Rupert. "How do you organize these get-togethers with your school friends?"

"That's simple. I have their contact information. The school is rather proud of the tradition of us staying in touch and keeping the old networks running."

"Do they post about it online? Maybe put the dates on an events calendar?"

"Ah! Well, they do, actually," Rupert said.

"That's how she knew. Meredith could have been monitoring the website and discovered that you had an upcoming event. How long has this been arranged?" I asked.

"We always fix the date of the next event a year in advance," Rupert said. "Everyone gets so busy. Once we figure out the date, we let the school know."

"And they led Meredith right to you," I said. "She contacted you a year ago, after she learned about your plans to meet."

"Four grown men against one woman?" Rupert shook his head. "I don't see it happening."

"Holly's right. It could work if she picked you off one by one," Alice said. "Kendal was an easy mark when he was rotten drunk and it was dark."

"And she tried with you," I said to Rupert. "She tried to mow you down with the buggy when she spotted you on your own."

"Do you really think she's been lurking in the shadows for days, hoping to kill us all?" Rupert shuddered.

"She's grieving and angry," Alice said. "She lost her son. Even if it was an accident, she can't move on."

"Should we tell the others?" Rupert said. "If their lives are at risk, we need to make sure they look out for each other."

"If they know about it, they won't act naturally," I said. "That might alert Meredith."

"Are you sure we shouldn't alert Campbell?" Alice ducked her head. "I know you don't like him much right now, but he is here to protect us."

"He'll think I'm making this up, as will the police. We need proof Meredith did this, or I'll still get blamed. If we involve Campbell, he'll charge in and take over. We might miss our only opportunity."

"Won't he be angry that we kept him in the dark?" Alice asked.

"Probably about as angry as I am for being accused of murder." I sighed when I saw the sad look on Alice's face. "We can tell him as soon as we have evidence against Meredith."

She nodded. "Okay, as long as he doesn't get angry with me."

I lifted my gaze to the sky. "I'll position myself at the back of the group when we're at the memorial garden. Alice, you go to the right side and make sure you've got a good view of the crowd. Keep a look out for Meredith and see if she's acting suspiciously or paying attention to anyone in the group. Rupert, you do the same, but stay at the front on the left. That way, we've got all the angles covered."

"I'll have to be at the front," Rupert said. "I'm giving a short speech before officially opening the memorial garden. I can certainly keep an eye on her from there."

"That will have to do," I said.

"Part of me really hopes you're wrong," Rupert said, "but I'm also very keen to find out who really killed Kendal. We must clear your name."

"That's what I'm hoping we'll do if we can catch Seb's mom in the act."

"We'd better get a move on," Alice said. "The crowd is gathering at the garden."

I nodded before we parted company and hurried into the kitchen.

"Is everything okay?" Chef Heston asked.

"The food's all done, ready for after the speeches at the garden. Would it be okay if I took a break now? I'd like to see the memorial garden when it's opened."

"You can have half an hour," he said. "But don't think you're going to be able to use this I've-almost-been-charged-with-murder-ruse to exploit my good nature for long."

"I promise, I have no plans to use this particular ruse again."

He grunted before turning away.

"I'll pass drinks around while I'm out there to keep people happy." I grabbed a tray of soft drinks, collected Meatball as extra backup, and hurried to the garden. I moved through the crowd, making sure I kept an eye on Meredith.

She was focused on the memorial garden, her hands clasped in front of her and a blank expression on her face.

Maybe I was wrong about her, and she was simply here to remember her lost son, but I had to be sure.

After ten minutes of wandering through the crowd, I knew exactly where all of Rupert's friends were. I moved to the back of the crowd. Alice was stood to the side. She gave me a big thumbs up and a smile.

She needed to work on her discreet sleuthing skills. She stuck out a mile in her long bright yellow dress.

Rupert stood at the front, patting his chest and shifting from foot to foot. He always got nervous at public events. I imagined he'd be even more nervous now there was a killer in the audience who had her sights set on him.

After a few more minutes of milling around, Rupert stepped to the front of the group. "Everybody, if I may have your attention. It's time to open the memorial garden at Audley Castle."

The crowd settled and pressed closer to hear him speak.

I half-listened as he extolled the virtues of the gardeners and the hard work that had gone into making the memorial garden a permanent feature.

I looked around, and my eyes widened. Alice was talking to Simon. She kept glancing over his shoulder at the crowd, but he was distracting her. She might miss Meredith making a move.

Although this situation wasn't terrible. If Simon was with Alice, that was one less person I'd need to keep a look out for and make sure Seb's mom wasn't going after him.

Meatball nudged my leg with his nose and whined.

"Is everything okay, boy?" I whispered.

"Woof." He pointed his nose toward the trees.

"We'll have a walk later. We're on an important mission right now," I said softly.

He nudged me again.

I glanced around, and my heart lurched. Christian was heading toward the trees. Not far behind him was Meredith.

I hurried after them, Meatball at my heels. Where was Christian going?

I hung back, making sure Meredith didn't spot me tailing her, but she was focused on following Christian and didn't look back.

Christian entered the woods first, and a moment later, Meredith followed. She wore a black rain jacket with a large hood. Her hands were stuffed in both pockets. It would be easy to conceal a weapon in those pockets, but there was no spade in evidence this time. If she was planning on killing Christian, I had no idea what she would use.

I crept through the trees, keeping an eye out for Christian or Meredith.

Meatball dashed ahead of me, and I was too slow to grab him. He paused by a tree and looked back, his tail wagging.

I hurried after him and ducked as I detected movement.

Christian and Meredith stood in a small clearing, facing each other.

I petted Meatball's head. "Good boy! You found them."

He licked my hand.

"This is a misunderstanding." Christian's words shot out of him. "I don't know what evidence you're talking about. Seb's death was an accident."

"You're wrong." Meredith's jaw looked tight.

Christian raised a hand. "I understand this is a difficult day. It's tough for me too. I was there at the lake. I saw it happen. Seb was my friend."

Meredith jabbed a finger at him. "You saw it happen, and you did nothing. The police showed me the reports. You goaded my son into swimming out of his depth and into danger."

"No! I mean, it was just a dare. We didn't do it because we wanted to hurt him." Christian ducked his head. "We all liked the guy."

"Sebastien told me he was bullied by you at school. He cried when I forced him to go back after the summer vacation. He said he couldn't face it anymore. The pressure was too much. I didn't listen. I insisted he go back. I sent him to his death. I sent him back to you and the people who were supposed to be his friends, and you killed him."

"You've got it all wrong. He just drowned."

"Sebastien didn't even like to swim. He wouldn't have been there if you and your gang of thugs hadn't forced him into it."

"We're not thugs." Christian glared at her. "You haven't got any evidence to prove otherwise. I'm sorry for your loss, but you're out of line. I'm leaving. The note you sent me was clearly a bluff. I only came here because I was curious."

So that was why Christian had ended up here. Meredith must have guilted him into meeting her.

"You're guilty," she said. "You coming here proves it. You're worried I have something on you and you'll finally go to prison, which is where you belong."

"I'm out of here," Christian said. "I won't say anything to the police on this occasion. I can see you're not in your right mind. Maybe you should get some professional help, though."

"You're not going anywhere." Meredith pulled a hand out of her pocket. She was holding a gun.

I gasped and stepped out from behind the tree I'd been using as cover. "Meredith! Stop!"

"Holly! What are you doing here?" She kept the gun on Christian as her panicked gaze swept to me.

"It was you, wasn't it?" I inched closer. "You murdered Kendal."

Her hand shook as she lifted her chin and stared at me. "I'm sorry you're taking the blame for that, but it's your own fault. When you moved the spade in the back of my car, I didn't have a chance to stop you. Before I could get rid of it, Campbell's team took the tools and fingerprinted them. I should have burned it, destroyed the evidence, but in a way, it helped me."

"You mean, you framed me."

"Only by accident," she said. "You're a decent person, Holly. I didn't want you implicated, but with the police looking at Izzie and then you, it gave me freedom to move around and plan my next move."

"What's going on?" Christian stared at me. "Are you in on this as well?"

I ignored him. "Meredith, don't do this. I understand how angry you are, and—"

"You understand nothing. Have you lost a child? Do you know what it feels like to have your heart ripped out because of the selfish actions of others? You have no clue what's going on in my head. I tried to convince the police to continue investigating what happened to Sebastien, but they said it was an accident. They let his friends get away with what they'd done because of their privileged positions. That was wrong."

I lifted a hand. "I get it. You're hurt and you want closure, but killing everyone who was at the lake that day isn't the answer."

Christian snorted a surprised laugh. "Lady, you need your head looking at. You—"

"You. Don't. Talk!" Meredith waved the gun at him. "This is the perfect solution for me. I was numb for such a long time after Sebastien's murder. I tried to rationalize it and convince myself that it was just one of those things. He was unlucky. Deep down, I knew that wasn't true. I put it all together over time. Real friends wouldn't have let that happen."

"Hold on," Christian said. "It really was an accident. We all felt bad about it."

"Liar! Sebastien deserves justice. He should be here. Instead, my only child was taken from me by his callous friends."

"This won't solve anything," I said. "Sebastien should be remembered in a positive way. The memorial garden will do just that. He'd hate for his friends to be killed by his mom."

Meredith blinked rapidly and scrubbed a hand down her face. "He was all I had. It was always just the two of us. His father was obsessed with work and never had any free time. Sebastien filled that hole in my life. When he was taken, I had nothing left."

"You have your memories of him," I said.

"Memories! They're not enough. I need to know I did everything I could to avenge his murder."

Christian sighed. "It wasn't murder. You're the only murderer around here." He glanced at me. "Did this crazy woman really kill Kendal?"

I shook my head at him. Now wasn't the time to start name calling. The way Meredith's arm was shaking, the gun could easily go off by accident.

"You shouldn't have followed me," Meredith said. "You're not a part of this. I was watching for the right time to deal with Lord Rupert and his friends."

"By separating them one by one and killing them all?" I said.

"Kendal first. I never did like that snot-nosed brat. Sebastien told me he was the ring leader of all the bullying when they were at school."

"What about Rupert?" I asked. "You tried to get him with the buggy."

"I couldn't miss the opportunity. When I saw him alone with his head in a book, he was asking for it."

"Then you wanted to kill Christian?" I asked.

She nodded. "He'd always acted suspiciously over what had happened to Sebastien. I knew that if I sent him a note, he wouldn't be able to resist coming to find out what I knew. That's a clear sign of guilt."

"Wrong. It's a sign that I cared about my old friend," Christian said.

"You're all terrible people. Each of you deserves what's coming to you." Meredith lifted the gun and aimed it at Christian's chest.

He backed up a few steps. "Wait! Let's talk about this. I can give you anything you want."

"I want my son back. Can you do that?" she snarled. "I thought not. Say goodbye."

A buzzing filled the air, and Meredith shrieked before her body convulsed.

Campbell emerged from behind a tree, holding a Taser.

Meredith groaned and slumped to the ground, the gun falling from her hand.

"How did you know we were here?" I stammered as Campbell hurried over to Meredith, followed by several members of his security team.

"Lord Rupert told me what was going on when he saw you running into the trees," he said. "You should have told me about your hare-brained plan before you even attempted it."

"I … I, well, I didn't think you'd believe me. You thought I was guilty of murder."

He grunted as he secured Meredith's arms behind her back. "Don't worry, Holly Holmes, I heard everything. You're in the clear."

Chapter 22

My lungs burned as I pushed to the top of the hill, two crates of cupcakes secured in the trolley on the back and Meatball wagging his tail from his secured position in the basket.

I zoomed past a row of pretty thatched cottages and inhaled the heady scent of honeysuckle. Who'd have thought, just two days ago, I was facing a murder charge? I'd also been faced with possible death, after foolishly confronting the woman who'd killed Kendal and attempted to murder Christian and Rupert.

Everything had moved so fast since that frightening afternoon.

I gasped as Rupert stepped out in front of me, his nose in a book. This time, I was ready. I dinged my bell and applied the brakes, coming to a stop just in time.

He looked around and smiled, completely unaware he'd been in any danger. That seemed to be his default position. "Holly! What brings you out of the castle?"

"Cake deliveries as usual," I said. "Good book?"

He held it up. "It was one of Sebastien's favorites. I thought I'd revisit it since he's been on my mind lately."

I wheeled the bike to the side of the road, hopped off, and walked alongside Rupert.

He petted Meatball on the head. "Smitherington's been updating me about the police investigation. Have you heard that Meredith's confessed to everything?"

I nodded. "She didn't have much choice, not with so many witnesses overhearing her confession."

"You were brave, Holly, chasing after her like that," Rupert said. "I wanted to come after you but didn't want to panic the crowd. I cut my speech short, found Campbell, and told him everything. I know that wasn't a part of the plan, but I was worried."

"Campbell filled me in after he'd marched Meredith away to the police. He also told me never to do anything as ridiculous as that again. I got a stern talking to. I've only just stopped shaking in fear."

"You should get a medal. If it wasn't for you, we'd have never figured it out. And heaven forbid, you may have been charged with a crime you weren't involved in."

"That would never have happened," I said. "I wasn't going down without a fight, and if that meant confronting Meredith to prove my innocence, that's what I was prepared to do."

"Did you know that she had a gun?"

"I figured she must have a weapon, but no, I didn't think she'd pull a gun out." If I had, I wouldn't have been so eager to chase after her.

"Smitherington told me the gun was her ex-husband's. She stole it from him. Meredith's been planning vengeance for a long time." He shuddered. "I feel sorry for her. I had no idea she held this bitterness against us. I can promise you this, Sebastien's death was an accident. We did everything we could to save him. Although ... if we hadn't encouraged him to swim in the first place, he'd still be here today."

"You can't blame yourself," I said. "It was a horrible, tragic accident. Meredith was too grief stricken to see that. This was her way of trying to get closure."

"Well, I'm jolly glad she failed." He grinned. "Did you hear that Izzie and Simon are dating again?"

"Wow! She's a fast worker. I guess she's not all that devastated about losing Kendal."

"I suspect she misses his social connections. He always went to the best parties, but that's about it."

"And your other friends have gone home?"

"Tony and Christian left this morning," he said. "It's back to normal now. In truth, I'm quite relieved. I know we have to do things for appearances' sake, but I don't enjoy their company. They're always bragging about how much money they make and the women they're dating."

Rupert was never a bragger, and he had the most to brag about, living in an enormous castle surrounded by luxury most of us would never experience.

We walked along in a companionable silence until I reached my first delivery stop.

"I, um, I keep meaning to ask you something." He stuffed his hands into his pants pockets and looked around.

"What's that?" A nervous tickle ran down my spine.

"It's just that, we get on well, don't we?"

"I like to think so," I said.

"Yes, me too. And—"

"There you are!" Alice raced across the road out of the Lady Belle Boutique and flung her arms around me. "My criminal best friend."

I chuckled as I stepped out of her embrace. "Steady on. What makes you think I'm a criminal?"

"I've heard all about your criminal past and the illegal marches and protests you went on with your granny. You naughty thing. She sounds like such fun. I imagine she'd get on well with Granny Philippa. We must arrange for them to meet."

I bit my bottom lip. "My gran's … unique. And she's not often around. I don't hear from her much." I got the occasional letter from prison, but she wasn't a big fan of writing.

"I insist you bring her to the castle as soon as you can. Granny Philippa gets lonely stuck in the turret. When she has too much time on her hands, she gets obsessed with her predictions. It'll do her the world of good to have a new, fun friend."

"The next time she gets in touch, I'll mention it to her." I wasn't sure how I felt about them meeting my gran. She was the serious black sheep of the family.

"Oh, and before I forget, there's a history exhibition we must visit on your next day off. You love the Tudors, and this is all about them. I find it all a bit stuffy and boring, but apparently, there'll be a talk on finding your distant family. It could be perfect for finishing off my own family tree. And you've still to get started on yours. We can get going on that after the exhibition."

"My family tree will take about five minutes to complete," I said. "But the exhibition sounds good. You should come too, Rupert."

Alice wrinkled her nose. "My brother isn't interested in that sort of thing."

"Oh, I wouldn't mind coming. Only if you want me there." He looked a little crestfallen.

I smiled warmly. "Of course you must come." A movement in the shadows caught my eye. Campbell was lurking in his usual discreet fashion, protecting the family.

I hadn't quite forgiven him for believing that I killed Kendal, but I understood why he'd pursued me. Campbell was logical minded. He followed the evidence, and there had been evidence to suggest I could have been the killer.

He nodded at me before retreating further into the shadows.

I happily listened as Alice continued to talk about the exhibition and all the fun it would be and that we'd have lunch and go shopping after the 'stuffy' exhibition.

I smiled up at Rupert, and he blushed before returning my grin.

"Why don't we ask Lady Philippa to the exhibition?" I asked. "You said she gets lonely. We could take her out for the day."

Rupert and Alice exchanged a loaded glance before she shook her head. "We have tried that a time or two, but it never ends well. The trouble with Granny Philippa is she's psychic."

My mouth dropped open. "That's a joke, right?"

Rupert shook his head. "It's an old family gift, apparently. Neither of us have it. Although my gut gets strange twinges from time to time."

"That's because you eat too much. You're such a piggy." Alice snorted before collapsing into giggles.

"I am not." Rupert glanced at me. "Well, maybe when it comes to Holly's cakes. That's the reason we lock Granny Philippa in the turret. It's for her own protection, and ours. We don't want the castle getting a bad reputation."

"The ghosts help out quite nicely with that." Alice continued to giggle. "A curse predicting granny will only make things worse."

I stared at them, still not sure whether my leg was being pulled.

My employers were on the weird side, especially Lady Philippa, who had been absolutely right about the murder and the trouble I'd face. But that had to be a one-off. Her predictions couldn't always come true.

Did I want to be a part of this? Live in a place that was possibly haunted, had a psychic granny locked in a turret, and a castle run by a family of eccentrics?

I took a deep breath as I looked around the beautiful village green, and the people walking by, and let the happy vibes float past.

I smiled. Yes, this was the life I wanted. Bring on the weird.

"Oooh! I've got a great idea. Let's help with your cake deliveries," Alice said. "It'll be such fun when people open their doors and they find Rupert and me standing outside. What a hoot. We might even get invited in for tea."

I grimaced. "I'm not sure about that."

"We can say it's an extra special delivery. A free visit from the Lord of the Manor." Alice prodded Rupert in the arm.

"Maybe you should listen to Holly," he said. "She has an important job to do."

Alice was already off with the first box of cakes in her hands. She strode to the wrong door and knocked loudly.

"Wait up, Alice. Not that house." As I raced to salvage the delivery, I couldn't help but smile.

This sure was an interesting life, and I was determined to enjoy every second of it.

About Author

K.E. O'Connor (Karen) is a cozy mystery author living in the beautiful British countryside. She loves all things mystery, animals, and cake (these often feature in her books.)

When she's not writing about mysteries, murder, and treats, she volunteers at a local animal sanctuary, reads a ton of books, binge watches mystery series on TV, and dreams about living somewhere warmer.

To stay in touch with the fun, clean mysteries, where the killer always gets their just desserts:

Newsletter: www.subscribepage.com/cozymysteries
Website: www.keoconnor.com/writing
Facebook: www.facebook.com/keoconnorauthor

Also By

Enjoy the complete Holly Holmes cozy culinary mysteries in paperback or e-book.

Cream Caramel and Murder

Chocolate Swirls and Murder

Vanilla Whip and Murder

Cherry Cream and Murder

Blueberry Blast and Murder

Mocha Cream and Murder

Lemon Drizzle and Murder

Maple Glaze and Murder

Read on for a peek at book two in the series - Chocolate Swirls and Murder!

Chapter 1

"Say you'll take part in the food fair baking contest." Princess Alice Audley strolled around the kitchen behind me as I prepared a tray of triple chocolate cupcakes for hungry café visitors.

"I'm too busy to consider the contest." I twirled chocolate icing over the cupcakes and passed them to Louise to go out to the café.

"You have a flair for making cakes look beautiful. I always tell people your food is a work of art." Alice had been buzzing around me like a cute, mildly annoying fly for ten minutes.

"Delicious works of art, I hope." I adjusted my grip on the tray of warm cinnamon buns I'd pulled out of the oven before placing it on the counter to cool.

Alice fluttered her naturally long dark lashes. "I'll be your best friend if you enter the contest."

I chuckled. Despite moving in radically different social circles, I considered Alice a really good friend. "Tourist season is in full swing. Chef Heston won't let me have the time off to prepare. And you know how fierce the competition will be. I'd have to bring my A game. No slacking off allowed."

"I'll order him to give you the time off." Alice jammed her hands on her hips and flipped her blonde hair over one shoulder with a toss of her head. "The public deserve to see how beautiful your cakes are. Plus, how delicious they are." She grabbed a cinnamon bun from the tray. "Ouch! That's hot."

I arched an eyebrow. "Ovens tend to do that to food. Leave them for a while. They won't be ready to ice for another half an hour, at least. And the frosting always brings out the cinnamon."

She pouted. "I want cake, and I want it now."

"Yes, your majesty." I dipped a quick curtesy before walking to the chiller cabinet. I took out a batch of fresh cream horns dipped in Belgian chocolate. "Have one of these."

"You see!" She held up the flaky pastry horn. "Perfection."

"Eat that and stop bothering me about the baking contest."

"But you'll be a huge success. Take some space on the Audley Castle stand on the day. You can sell your cupcakes to see how much people love your desserts," Alice said. "That will liven things up. We only ever have boring information on there about our castle and my dusty old ancestors. That's yawn city for most people. However, if you entice them with luscious treats they can buy, you'll see how popular you are. Then you'll want to enter the contest."

Every year, Audley Castle held a fantastic food fair. Vendors came from all over the country to sell delicious treats to visitors. It had been running for over fifty years. This year, there was a full day of selling, followed by three days of competition, with the best bakers and cooks fighting it out with perfect pies and cakes to win in different categories, plus, an overall grand winner.

"Holly Holmes! I insist upon it." Alice wagged a finger at me. "You know what I do to people who don't follow my orders."

"Threaten to chop off their heads?" Sometimes, those threats sounded a bit too real.

A peal of laughter shot out of her mouth. "That's right. You can't deprive the world of your treats. The Duke and Duchess are even judging this year."

"It doesn't feel right that I enter," I said. "I work here."

"That doesn't disqualify you from entering," Alice said. "I've checked the rules. Besides, it's all judged fairly. Please say you'll enter."

"Maybe next year."

"Chef Heston!" Alice hurried over as my grumpy boss entered the kitchen and grabbed hold of his arm, dragging him toward me. "You have to tell Holly to help on the castle stand at the food fair and enter the competition. She must take part."

"Must she now." His dark eyes narrowed as he glared at me. "Trying to get out of work again, Holmes?"

I lifted my hands and shook my head. "I've already told Princess Alice that I'm too busy in the kitchen."

"And I've told her it's her civic duty to share her treats with everyone," Alice said. "There's plenty of room on the Audley Castle display stand. And we're short of people to look after it. This is the perfect solution. Holly can do a few hours and sell delicious treats. She can also send people to the café, so it's a win-win all round."

Some people thought Alice was nothing but an extremely beautiful face surrounded by a mass of dazzling blonde curls. She was nothing short of a genius when she wanted to be.

Chef Heston grunted. "We'll be busy during the food fair. People still come to the café, especially if they've been looking around for several hours and need somewhere to sit."

"You can spare Holly," Alice said. "Look at all the cakes she's already baked today. And you've got a whole team working here. You won't miss her."

I gritted my teeth. I sort of hoped he would, or he might decide I was superfluous to requirements and get rid of me.

"Will you promote the café if you do this?" he asked me.

"Of course," I said. "I can put out samples of what we have at the café. And I'll sell our cakes as well."

"And you must get her to take part in the competition," Alice said.

"Hmmm. I'm not sure about that. That will take her away from her duties," Chef Heston said.

"Don't be such a meanie!" Alice swatted his arm.

I masked a smile behind my hand. Only a princess could get away with doing that. "I don't mind not being a part of the competition." Although if I did enter, I might test out a Neapolitan and red velvet layer cake with a chocolate chip mousse.

"You do have those unusual flourishes you add to your creations," Chef Heston said. "It would be interesting to see what other people thought of them."

"That's a yes!" Alice stood on her tiptoes and kissed Chef Heston's cheek.

He flushed bright pink before turning and hurrying away.

"I'll pay for that," I said. "You bullied him into getting me involved."

Alice's eyes glittered as she beamed at me. "So, what are you going to bake?"

I grinned back, enthused by her excitement. "Well, I was thinking of—"

The kitchen door opened. Lord Rupert Audley bumbled in, smiling when he saw me. "I was hoping you might have some of your triple chocolate fudge brownies available. I've been thinking about them all morning. In fact, I had a dream about one last night."

"Some came out of the oven ten minutes ago," I said. "They're still warm."

Rupert pushed his messy blond hair out of his face. "They're perfect like that. Not that they aren't delicious at any other time. You always bake perfection."

"You can't beat a just out of the oven brownie." I plated one up and handed it over.

"I'm glad you're here." Alice bit into her cream horn. "I'm twisting Holly's arm to get her involved in the cake contest. She's pretending she doesn't have enough time. I know you can convince her otherwise."

"Well, you do make jolly delicious cakes," he said. "If I had a vote, I'd vote for you to win the whole thing."

My cheeks grew warm, and I looked away. "That's kind of you. However, as I was explaining to your sister—"

"Stuff and nonsense," Alice said. "Besides, it's too late. I've put your name down."

"You've done what?" I stared at her in disbelief.

She grinned and ate more cream horn. "It's all arranged."

"What if I'd said no?"

"I knew you wouldn't." Alice giggled.

I bit my bottom lip. I was secretly excited about being a part of this contest. I had four main loves in my life: my adorable corgi cross, Meatball, who was currently lounging in his kennel outside the kitchen; my interest in history; my love of new fitness trends; and baking. It wasn't so long ago that I ran my own café. It didn't end well, but I loved nothing more than starting the day with my head full of recipes to tempt people with.

Chef Heston returned and loudly cleared his throat. "This is a kitchen I'm trying to run here, not a social event."

Alice giggled again before grabbing her brother's arm. "We're going." She winked at me before they left the kitchen.

Chef Heston shook his head. "There's a delivery you need to do."

"Where to?" I asked.

"Mrs. Brown."

"Is the van free?"

He smirked. "Take the bike. The exercise will do you good. I noticed you've been sampling your own brownies again."

My eyes widened. "Taste testing is an important part of the job."

He snorted a laugh. "The bike's outside waiting for you."

I repressed a sigh as I took off my apron and headed outside with the four boxes of cakes for Mrs. Brown. Chef Heston loved to torture me by insisting I ride the delivery bike into Audley St. Mary.

Not that it was a huge chore, unless the trolley really was loaded with cake. But Audley St. Mary had a few hills, and I always ended up puffed out and sweaty by the time my deliveries were over.

I hadn't had time to take Meatball for a walk at lunchtime, we'd been so rushed with orders, so once the cakes were secured on the trolley, I hurried around to his kennel.

He bounced up as soon as he saw me and wagged his little brown tail. He was my best friend, and it had been a condition of me taking this job that I could bring him with me. And, although quite rightly, Meatball wasn't allowed in the kitchen, I'd been given permission to erect a luxurious kennel right outside the door so I could keep an eye on him while I worked.

"Come on, boy," I said. "Delivery time."

"Woof woof." That was his version of saying yes. He waited patiently as I attached his harness and helmet—safety first—before lifting him into the wicker basket secured on the front of the bike.

Yes, it was that kind of bike. Old-fashioned, heavy-framed, and with no gears. It was part of the image Audley Castle portrayed. We had a lot of traditions at the castle and apparently using bikes with no gears was one of them.

I headed away from the castle and made my way up and down the first hill. By the time I'd reached Mrs. Brown's thirty minutes later, I was out of breath and my legs felt like they'd gotten a workout.

I climbed off the bike, lifting a hand in greeting as several residents wandered past.

Audley St. Mary was a small, friendly village. The village had grown up around Audley Castle and was proud to have mostly independent stores and a wonderful history that dated back hundreds of years.

I petted Meatball on the back before untying the cake boxes and walking along the pretty cottage garden pathway to Mrs. Brown's front door.

She lived in a tiny thatched cottage on the edge of the village. As far as I knew, she lived alone, and rumor had it she had more money than the Queen.

I knocked at the door.

Mrs. Brown's wrinkled face lit up as she opened it and saw the cakes. "Holly! You're my savior. When I contacted the kitchen yesterday to put in my last-minute request, I wasn't sure you'd have time for me." She gestured me into the cottage.

"We've always got time for you, Mrs. Brown."

She smiled. "I'd forgotten all about the supper gathering I'm hosting this evening. My eight friends and I have been getting together for almost fifty years. Once a month, we take turns to host a small party. It must be my age making me forget. I only remembered because I was chatting to Dorothy on the phone last night and she said 'see you tomorrow'. I pretended that I knew what she meant. It was only when I consulted my diary that it came flooding back. Never get old, Holly." She patted my hand.

I wouldn't mind being as sprightly as Mrs. Brown when I was in my eighties. She was independent, got out of her cottage several times a week, and I'd even seen her at the village Pilates class.

I set the cakes on the wooden kitchen counter. "These should ensure the party gets off to a good start."

"Absolutely. Let's take a peek." She lifted a box lid and sighed in delight. "Your cakes are so pretty. I always know when you've baked them. Look at those tiny flowers on the top. They're so beautiful, I feel guilty eating them."

I chuckled, pleased she'd noticed my careful eye for detail. "Please do eat them. I'd be offended if you didn't."

"Oh! Of course. It'll be my pleasure. We plan to eat every last one. Although I did order an extra box so I could enjoy some later in the week." She closed the box lid and studied me in silence for a few seconds. "Do you see anything of Lady Philippa while you're at the castle?"

"Of course. She's got a sweet tooth and is often asking for cakes to be sent to her room. I sometimes take them if we're busy in the kitchen."

"Oh! Is she unwell? She can't leave her bedroom?" Mrs. Brown's age-spotted hand fluttered against her narrow chest.

"No, nothing like that. She tends to spend most of her time in the east turret. She likes it up there. It's got a good view of the grounds." I deliberately didn't mention that

Lady Philippa believed her family kept her locked in there. "Do you know her?"

Mrs. Brown looked out the window. "We used to be friends. Every time I have one of these gatherings, I wonder if I should rekindle our friendship."

"Did you have a falling out?"

She looked back at me and her gaze hardened. "I should say. At one of our tea parties, she declared that somebody was about to die. I was mortified. How can you have a fun party when someone just declared a death is about to occur?"

My eyes widened. It wasn't the first time I'd heard about Lady Philippa's ability to predict the future, especially when it came to somebody's demise. "Did the person die?"

"Yes! That's the worst thing. Because of her unfortunate ability, it was set in stone."

"Her … ability?"

"Oh yes! And you must have heard that the Audleys, and those who marry into the family, become cursed," Mrs. Brown said. "A love curse so I've heard. The rumors are only fueled by the fact they live in a haunted castle."

"I don't know about ghosts." I'd experienced my fair share of spooky noises and cold spots but wasn't ready to admit there might be ghosts in the place I worked. "It can get a bit drafty in there, though."

"Drafty!" Mrs. Brown shook her head. "You'd be wise to keep an open mind. Lady Philippa and that whole family have mystery surrounding them. No, I think it's better if I keep my distance. If I invite her to another party, she'll only do something dramatic. That would be the end of my social life."

"Yes, I suppose it might. Well, I'd better get going," I said, not sure I was in a position to advise on such a delicate matter. "Busy day at the castle. Lots of baking to do."

"Of course." Mrs. Brown led me back to the door, tucking a ten pound note in my hand as she did so. "Buy yourself something nice."

"Thanks." I smiled and nodded. The tips were amazing from the wealthy villagers. They all went into my fund to buy new recipe books and go on cooking courses.

"And it's the food fair soon. I trust you'll be taking part."

"I wasn't until about an hour ago. I'll be on the Audley Castle stand if you want to drop by."

"With free samples?" She opened the door, a hopeful glint in her eyes.

"Of course." I smiled and waved goodbye as I headed back to the bike. Everyone seemed to know about the curses and hauntings at the castle. It wasn't such a surprise. The tourist brochure and the website played up to the fact the place was supposed to be haunted. And I'd experienced first-hand how spookily accurate Lady Philippa's predictions could be.

I unclipped Meatball's helmet and took him for a fifteen-minute walk around the village green before we headed back and I grabbed the bike. I turned it toward Audley Castle and cycled back as fast as I could.

I had a lot of work to do if I was entering this cake competition. Bakers could be a competitive bunch as we tried to outdo each other with the lightest sponge and sweetest buttercream. I needed to get testing and baking if I was to stand a chance of winning.

I'd only just settled Meatball back in his kennel and walked into the kitchen to wash up when Chef Heston caught me.

"You're late."

"I took the delivery to Mrs. Brown, and she wanted to chat. It would have been rude not spend a few minutes with a lonely old lady."

"Sure it would." He scowled at me. "Lady Philippa has been asking for you. Take this up to her rooms immediately." He handed me a tea tray with a pink flowered teapot, china tea cups, and four strawberry scones with clotted cream and strawberry preserves.

"I'll get right on that." I gulped down my sudden nerves. The east turret was never my favorite place.

Mrs. Brown's comments about the castle being haunted were front and center of my mind as I walked through my first cold spot. It was nothing. This was an ancient castle, built in Jacobean times. Cracks would appear over the years and the cold would get in. That's all it was.

I shoved away my fears and dashed up the spiral staircase to the east turret rooms.

"Holly Holmes! Where have you been?" Lady Philippa spoke before she could even see me as I hurried past the large leaded windows toward her lounge.

"Sorry I'm late. I got here as quickly as I could." I nudged the door open with my hip and entered the room. It was an opulent living space, with expensive velvet curtains draped around the windows, red silk wallpaper, and luxurious designer furniture scattered around the room. Lady Philippa also had a huge bedroom with an ornate four poster bed. I had no idea how they'd gotten it up the spiral staircase. Maybe it had been built in place.

"You've been on my mind." Lady Philippa gestured to a side table by the high-backed chair she sat in. "Pour me a cup of tea. I'm parched."

"Of course. Why have you been thinking about me?"

"Because of who you've been to visit." She was dressed in a demure beige silk dress, diamonds glittering around her neck. "You've been gossiping about me."

I looked up hurriedly as I handed her a tea cup. "I wouldn't say gossiping." How did she know Mrs. Brown had been discussing her less than two hours ago?

"My gut never lies," she said. "And I smell lavender. Olivia Brown always wore a lavender perfume."

My mouth dropped open.

"Stop trying to catch flies, girl. Sit down and sort those scones. Remember, I like my preserves under my cream."

I snapped my mouth shut and dealt with the scones before handing her two on a plate.

"The rest are for you," she said. "I imagine you've worked up an appetite cycling to the village and back with those cakes for Olivia and her gaggle of wrinkled old girlfriends."

I glanced at the binoculars on the window ledge and smiled. "Have you been busy birdwatching again?"

She grinned. "I'm a keen birdwatcher. There's always something fascinating outside to keep me occupied. So, what has Olivia been gossiping about?"

"Nothing bad about you. She was saying that she knew you, and you used to go to her parties."

Her grin faded, and she nodded. "We used to be close. She was a real firecracker. All the men fell in love when they saw Olivia and those raven curls."

"She's not raven haired anymore," I said.

Lady Philippa patted her professionally dyed and styled bobbed hair. "None of us are the same as we used to be. How is she?"

"Doing well from what I can tell," I said.

"She still has that little cottage?"

"That's right." I bit into my scone. The perfect combination of cream and sweet strawberry preserves made me sigh in pleasure.

"She never married. Back in our heyday, marriages were often arranged, especially in the upper classes. It helped cement relationships and forge business deals. I can't think of anything worse. Olivia got several proposals of marriage, and her family tried to set her up on numerous occasions, but she comes from a moneyed background and inherited the lot when her parents died. She never found anyone to love. Good for her, living a life she always wanted without being saddled with some weak-chinned wonder who'd bore her to death."

"She might miss you," I said cautiously. "She was interested in how you were doing."

Lady Philippa gave a most unladylike snort. "I doubt that very much. Did she tell you why I stopped going to her parties?"

"Something about predicting a death?"

"Exactly! She shunned me for telling the truth." She shook her head. "One second, we were all laughing and joking, then I announced my prediction and it all went wrong. Olivia said she was feeling unwell and everyone had to leave. The next week, I wandered past her cottage and they were all together. Olivia didn't invite me back after that."

"Maybe it's time to mend that bridge," I said. "It could be fun to host a few parties here for your friends."

She waved a hand in the air as if to dismiss the idea. "Too much has happened since then. It would be like strangers meeting. We'd have nothing to say to each other."

"True friendship isn't like that. I have friends I only see once a year, but it's like we've never been apart. We just pick up a conversation and off we go."

"Hmmm. Lucky you."

"Don't you get lonely up in this turret on your own?"

"If my family didn't keep me locked up here, I'd be free to make new friends," she said with a dramatic sigh. "Anyway, I didn't call you up here to gossip about my former friends. I want to talk about the death I see in the very near future."

Chocolate Swirls and Murder is available to buy in paperback or e-book format.

ISBN: 978-1-9163573-1-0

Here's one more treat. Enjoy this delicious recipe for caramel drizzled muffins. Meatball and Princess Alice approved!

Recipe – Delicious Caramel Drizzled Muffins

Prep time: 10 minutes **Cook time:** 20 minutes

A one-bowl recipe to give you delicious, moist, moreish muffins. Can be kept in a tin for 4 days or in the freezer for 3 months.

Recipe can be made dairy and egg-free. Substitute milk for a plant/nut alternative, use dairy-free spread, and mix 3 tbsp flaxseed with 1 tbsp water to create a flax 'egg' as a binding agent.

INGREDIENTS
1/4 cup (57g) unsalted butter, melted
1 cup (227g) buttermilk
1 large egg
1/4 cup (57g) canola or vegetable oil
1 teaspoon vanilla extract
1 tablespoon caramel extract
1 cup (227g) light brown sugar – use less if you don't have a sweet tooth
2 cups plus 2 tablespoons (270g) of all-purpose flour
1 teaspoon baking soda

1 teaspoon cinnamon

Salted caramel, for drizzling (I use store bought Hershey's or Carnation)

INSTRUCTIONS

1. Preheat oven to 350F (180C) Line a 12-cup muffin pan with paper cases or use silicone.

2. In a large bowl, melt the butter in microwave and set to one side.

3. In a medium bowl, add the buttermilk, oil, egg, vanilla, caramel and mix.

4. Add this mixture to the melted butter and whisk briefly.

5. Add the brown sugar and combine.

6. Add the flour, baking soda, cinnamon, and stir. Don't overmix. The batter will be lumpy (this is fine.)

7. Add batter to muffin pan – ¾ full only.

8. Bake for 18 - 20 minutes until tops are domed and a toothpick comes out clean.

9. Allow muffins to cool for 10 minutes before removing.

10. Drizzle with salted caramel sauce. Don't add the caramel until you're ready to eat to avoid a soggy bottom.